"SHUT UP AND LISTEN!"

The voice on the phone struck terror in his heart. He was trembling with the effort, but he shut up and listened.

"There's a ferry leaving Vineyard Haven at 1:45 P.M. You'd better be on that ferry. When you get off at Woods Hole, drive straight to Providence. There's a restaurant called The Blue Viking. Your daughter will be waiting there. When you pick her up, go straight back to New York. Forget about Martha's Vineyard and don't ever come back. Have you got that?"

"Yes."

"And one more thing, Blake. If there's any hitch, any tricks on your part, you'll never see your daughter again . . ."

Other Avon Books by
Ed McBain

BIG MAN
BREAD
CALYPSO
DEATH OF A NURSE
DOLL
EIGHT BLACK HORSES
80 MILLION EYES
GANGS!
GUNS
HAIL TO THE CHIEF
HE WHO HESITATES
ICE
KILLER'S CHOICE
LIGHTNING
LONG TIME NO SEE
LULLABY
THE MUGGER
POISON
THE SENTRIES
TRICKS
VANISHING LADIES
VESPERS
WHERE THERE'S SMOKE

Coming Soon

RUNAWAY
WIDOWS

EVEN THE WICKED

ED McBAIN

Originally published under
the pseudonym Richard Marsten

AVON BOOKS NEW YORK

This work was originally published under the pseudonym Richard Marsten.

This is a work of fiction. The people and the incidents were all invented by the author.

AVON BOOKS
A division of
The Hearst Corporation
1350 Avenue of the Americas
New York, New York 10019

Published by arrangement with HUI Corporation
Library of Congress Catalog Card Number: 91-92068
ISBN: 0-380-71122-2

First Avon Books Printing: December 1991

Printed in the U.S.A.

RA 10 9 8 7 6 5 4 3 2 1

This is for Bob and Fay

1

THEY BOARDED THE FERRY TOGETHER AT WOODS HOLE, the tall man with the brown hair and eyes, and the nine-year-old blonde who was his daughter. They sat together on the front seat of the Plymouth, and the dock boards squeaked a little as the car crossed them, and then the high vault of the ferry swallowed the car and the man followed the frenzied hand directions of the attendant, keeping to the right, pulling the Plymouth up behind a Cadillac.

This was the first time his daughter had been on a boat, and he could see her eyes reflected in the windshield, wide, and brown, and very frightened. Her hands were clutched over the small purse in her lap. She wore a blue cotton dress with a flare skirt, and a bright blue ribbon caught her hair into a golden ponytail. She looked very mature and very dressed-up but nevertheless very frightened. He put one hand over the hands on her purse.

"A penny for Penny's," he whispered, and a smile magically appeared on her mouth, the cheeks suddenly dimpling. It was her smile that bore the closest resemblance, he realized, her sudden radiant smile. It was her smile that struck deep inside, struck to a vulnerable sensitive core which layers and layers of practiced hardness could never cover. For a moment, the smile registered in his brown eyes, tracing them with pain. For a moment, memory swirled from the high overhead of the ferry, rushed into darkened corners of the automobile, drifted into raw corners of his mind.

He tried to shut it out. Deliberately, coldly, he tried to

shut it out. He was here because of a memory, but the memory could not be served if he allowed it to affect his thinking. The thinking had to be cold and rational, concise and pure. The thinking . . .

A head appeared at Penny's window. A politely nonintrusive smile preceded the voice.

"Would you turn off your motor, sir, and please pull up the hand brake?"

"Sure," he said. His voice was deep and well modulated, instantly recognizable as a trained voice. He watched the attendant as he moved away from the car, working his way forward, repeating the same message at each parked automobile. Had this man been on the ferry last year too? He could not remember.

"He had freckles all over his face," Penny said.

"That's Freckles Malachy," he answered. "Didn't you know?" He watched her face blossom with delight, become instantly alert, the eyes bright and expectant.

"Tell me about Freckles," she said.

"On the way topside," he said. "Come on, honey." He turned off the engine, and hoisted her out of the car. She took his hand the moment her feet touched the deck again. Together, they threaded their way through the parked cars, moving toward the forward ladder.

"What about Freckles?" she reminded him.

He began the story. The Malachy stories always began the same way, and they always ended the same way. It was their pattern, perhaps, which delighted the child. Mary had started the pattern one night four years ago, when Penny had been only five, when they'd still lived in Stuyvesant Town. The first Malachy story had been about Uncle Mike Malachy, a robust fellow who could hold his breath under water for an incredible twelve hours.

"Once upon a time," Mary had said, "in the family called Malachy, here was a man named Uncle Mike Malachy."

That had been the beginning. He had stood in the doorway to Penny's room and watched his wife as she told her imaginative tale, the single light on the dresser spinning her hair into an airy web of glistening gold. She had gone on for fifteen minutes while Penny listened breathlessly, and then she had ended her story with the words which later formed the closing pattern for all stories: "And Uncle Mike Malachy—and *all* the Malachys—lived happily ever after."

All the Malachys, he thought now—but not the Blakes. Not Mary Blake, and not Zachary Blake, and maybe not even Penny Blake. Unconsciously, he tightened his grip on her small hand.

"Once upon a time," he said, "in the family called Malachy, there was a boy named Freckles Malachy."

"Was he a cousin?" Penny asked.

"Yes, he was a cousin," Zach said.

"Then his name was *Cousin* Freckles Malachy, wasn't it?"

"Yes," he said. "It was Cousin Freckles Malachy."

"What did he do, Daddy?"

"He had the brightest, most gleaming freckles of anybody in the world," he said, "but the freckles made him very sad . . ."

The ferry was under way. It nosed out of the slip and headed into Vineyard Sound. Zach talked to his daughter while they climbed to the upper deck. He found a chair for them, and then continued his story. And twenty minutes later, he ended the story with the pattern Mary had set so long ago, and he sat with his arms around the little girl, and watched the gulls overhead, and each time they shrieked they seemed to echo a single agonizing word.

And the word was *Mary.*

The island of Martha's Vineyard looked forbidding.

It had not looked that way a year ago. Even looking back at the island when he was leaving, even after what had happened, even knowing what dread cargo the ferry had carried below, it had not seemed as forbidding then as it looked now. Perhaps it was the day. Perhaps the gray mists which shrouded the island were not what he'd expected.

There had been sunshine last summer, a month of incredibly bright sunshine which he'd shared with his wife on what they'd called their second honeymoon, even though they'd never really had a true first honeymoon. But for this trip alone, they had left Penny with her grandmother Blake, and they'd gone to Martha's Vineyard because they'd heard it was a place untouched by time, a place of crashing surf and silent inland ponds, a place of lonely beach roads, of winging slender terns and crying flocks of gulls—a place away from the rat race.

He had, the last summer, just been a part of the biggest scramble in the history of television, a no-holds-barred, tooth-and-nail struggle for Resignac's biggest broadcasting plum. Ed Liggett, the relentless interviewer who'd parlayed television's deadliest half-hour into a commodity sponsors screamed for, had gone network. And in going network, he had left the interviewer's chair open, and there wasn't a performer at Resignac Broadcasting—either in radio or television—who didn't want the job.

Zach got it.

It took a lot to get it. It always takes a lot to get something you really want. And then, after what happened on the Vineyard, he didn't want it any more. He told both his bosses. He told Resenwald first, and then he told DeBoignac. They understood, they said. They gave him back his old 6:15 P.M. radio news commentary spot. He supposed now that he had thrown away the opportunity of a lifetime. His face could have become as well known as Ed Liggett's. But at the time, he had not wanted to present his face to anyone. He wanted only a dark quiet corner, wanted only the anonymity of a radio microphone.

The boat edged into the slip at Vineyard Haven.

Zach and Penny went back to the car and waited their turn to disembark. The dock was loaded with cars and people. Women waved at arriving guests. Men in Bermuda shorts extended welcoming hands. Alongside the wood-paneled ferry waiting room, a man had set up an easel, and he painted a view of the Sound, oblivious to the crowd, his head bobbing from painting to water and back again. The Plymouth came off the boat and onto the dock. The Cadillac pulled to one side, waiting for the island infidels to clear the dock and the town before heading for the pined-and-moneyed exclusivity of West Chop. The Edgartown cocktail-and-regatta set were making their turns, cars brimming with guests. Zach turned the Plymouth in the opposite direction, heading up-island.

"It's nice, Daddy," Penny said. "Are we staying here?"

"We're going up-island," he told her. "To Menemsha."

"Like Menemsha Skulnik?" she asked.

"This Menemsha is Indian," he said.

"Really? Are there Indians here, Daddy?"

"Out at Gay Head there are."

Penny considered this solemnly for a moment. Then she said, "Was it the Indians who killed Mommy?"

The question startled him. In his own grief, he had not imagined the child thought much about it.

"No," he said. "Mommy drowned."

Almost as if she were thinking aloud, Penny said, "Mommy was a good swimmer."

"Yes," he answered. "Mommy was a good swimmer."

2

THE HOUSES ON MARTHA'S VINEYARD ARE ALMOST UNIformly gray.

The shingles weather quickly, buffeted by water and wind, until they attain the silvery hue of a dowager's hair, and then they seem to stop. Gray was the color that day. Gray shingled houses, and a gray sky, and gray waters lapping inland marshes, rolling in grayly against the shore beaches. The only sunshine that day was the burst of Penny's hair in the car beside him.

He had rented the Menemsha cottage from a woman named Carol Dubrow, a real estate agent in Chilmark. He had met her briefly the summer before when Mary and he had stopped at her place to pick up the key to the house. He had spoken to her yesterday on the phone, and his memory of the woman had been fortified by the solid ring of her voice. Mrs. Dubrow was in her late sixties, a formidable woman with iron-gray hair and a steel rod down the center of her back. Her eyes were as green as the ocean, and her mouth was a trap rivaling that of any clam in the salt water marshes. She was a tall, spare woman, as weathered as the gray shingles which covered the house she owned.

When Zach pulled into the Dubrow driveway, Penny asked, "Is this our house?"

"No," he said. "I've got to get the key. Want to come inside?"

"I'll wait in the car," she said. She leaned over the back seat, picked up a comic book, and was absorbed in it instantly. Zach climbed the steps to the front porch, stopped before the screen door, looked for a bell and, finding none, knocked.

"Come in," a girl's voice called.

He opened the screen door.

"In here," the voice said. "Back of the house."

He walked through a cool, dim corridor, past an old table with a wired kerosene lamp on it. The house felt moist, the way only an island house can feel on a bad day. He could almost taste salt in the musty air.

The girl was sitting at a desk set into an alcove just outside the kitchen. She sat quite erect at the desk, rapidly writing. She looked up, and he saw the same sea-green eyes that belonged to Mrs. Dubrow. But these eyes were set in an oval face framed with hair as black as sin, as short as virtue. The eyes studied him candidly.

"Yes?" she said.

She was wearing a denim shirt and dungaree trousers, but neither disguised the complete femininity of her body. Looking at her, he tried to decide how old she was, figured she couldn't be more than nineteen.

"I'm here for the Fielding house key," he said.

"The Fielding house," she repeated. She opened the top drawer of the desk. He could see a clutter of tagged keys in the open drawer. She poked among the keys and then lifted a yellow-tagged one out of the pile. The word FIELDING was lettered on the tag. She handed him the key.

"There you are, Mr. Carpenter," she said.

"The name's Blake," he told her, and he turned to go.

"Hey! Wait a minute!"

He looked at her. "What's the matter?"

"What did you say your name was?"

"Blake. Zach Blake."

"That's what I thought you said. You'd better give me that key."

"What for?"

"The Fielding house was rented to Mr. Carpenter, that's what for," she said. Her voice carried complete conviction. She was stating something very plain and very logical. He would have given her the key had he not spoken to Mrs. Dubrow yesterday and wired her $500 immediately afterwards.

"Where's Mrs. Dubrow?" he said.

"She's on vacation."

"Where?"

"Boston."

"When did she leave?"

"This morning."

"And who are you?"

"Anne Dubrow. Her daughter."

"Well, Miss Dubrow, I wired your mother $500 for the Fielding house yesterday morning. If you'll check—"

"Give me the key," she said.

"I paid for this key. Check your—"

"I don't have to check. Our salesman rented the Fielding house to Mr. Carpenter this morning. Went all the way to New Bedford on the ferry to take the deposit. Mr. Carpenter's got the house until Labor Day."

"Is he here now?"

"No, he's in New Bedford. Won't get here until the day after tomorrow."

"How much of a deposit did he give?"

"Half the full rental."

"And how much is that?"

"The full rental is $1500. He gave our salesman $750."

"Well, you'd better give it back to him," Zach said patiently. "I called your mother from New York yesterday. I told her I wanted the Fielding house for two weeks, and she said the price was $500. I told her that was a bit steep, but she said she usually rented it for the full season and my wanting it for two weeks would put the kibosh on that, hence the somewhat high—"

"My mother doesn't talk like that."

"The language is mine, Miss Dubrow, but the meaning is hers. In any case, I wired her five hundred bucks at eleven o'clock yesterday morning. I don't know who Mr.

Carpenter of New Bedford is, but he'll have to find himself another house. Good-by."

She came after him with remarkable swiftness, catching his arm and then whirling him to face the blazing sea-green eyes.

"Just a second, mister!" she said, and he had the feeling she was about to hit him.

"Miss Dubrow—"

"Give me that key," she said.

"We're being pretty damn foolish, aren't we? All you've got to do is check your records. You'll see—"

"All right, come on back in here," she said. "I know you're lying, but just to satisfy you, I'll—"

"I'm not in the habit of being called a liar by a nineteen-year-old kid," Zach said, annoyed. "I'll wait until you check, but—" He stopped. Anne Dubrow was smiling. "What the hell's so funny?"

"What you said. I'll be twenty-four next week."

"Happy birthday," he said. "Let's get this thing settled."

They went back to the desk together. She sat behind it and opened a small account book. He spotted his name in it before she did.

"There it is," he said. "Zachary Blake."

"Yes," she said. She had begun biting her lip. "I guess Pete made a mistake," she said. "This is terrible."

"Who's Pete?"

"Pete Rambley, mother's salesman. I guess he didn't know the Fielding house had already been rented." Her eyes were getting troubled. "What do we do now?"

"You call this Mr. Carpenter, whoever he is, and tell him somebody goofed. Tell him you've got another house for him. Tell him—"

"I couldn't do that."

"Why not?"

"He wants the Fielding house."

"So do I. And I've got priority."

"But it's such a big house," she said. "Are you here with a lot of people or—"

"Just my nine-year-old daughter," Zach said, "and she's probably been kidnaped from the car by now. I don't see what difference the size of my party ma—"

"I thought you might take another house."

"I want *this* house."

"Is your wife with you? Could I speak to her?"

The room was suddenly very still. He could hear bird noises coming from the woods behind the house. He looked at the girl steadily and very slowly said, "My wife drowned in Menemsha Bight last summer."

The girl seemed shocked for a moment. "Oh," she said. "Blake. Of course. Mary Blake."

"Yes."

"I'm sorry." She lowered her eyes.

"That's all right. May I go now?"

"Well . . . well, I don't know what to do, Mr. Blake." She was still staring at the open book, as if unwilling to meet his eyes now that she knew about his wife. "Mr. Carpenter's coming the day after tomorrow. What shall I tell him?"

"That's your problem," he said. "I don't know, and frankly I don't give a damn."

The green eyes flashed up at him with unexpected ferocity. "You're a pretty bitter person, aren't you?" Anne Dubrow said.

"Yes," he answered. "I am. Are we finished?"

"We're finished," she said. "Enjoy your stay."

He turned his back to her and walked out to the car. Penny looked up from her comic book.

"Did you get the key?" she asked.

"Yep."

He started the car, and began to drive to Menemsha.

There is no going back. One should never go back.

He realized that the instant he saw the house. He drove the car up the rutted sand road and then pulled into the parking space, and the gray shingles of the house reached out to engulf him. Mary was with him again in that moment, sitting beside him, her eyes opening wide in delight as she saw the house and the ocean vista behind it. He could almost hear her voice, almost hear the car door slamming, the sound of her feet on the packed sand as she ran to the back of the house and the porch that overlooked the water.

"Is that it?" Penny asked.

"What?" He turned slowly, staring at her.

"Is this—?"

"Yes," he said. "Yes."

She stared at him. "Does it make you sad, Daddy?"

"Yes, darling," he said. "It makes me very sad." He clutched her to him suddenly, holding her fiercely, feeling fresh pain, squeezing his eyes shut tightly. She drew away from him slowly and then looked into his face with the wide-open candor of a very young child.

"Why did we come here, Daddy?" she asked.

And because there was honesty on her face and in her eyes, and because he had never lied to his daughter in the short nine years of her life, he held her eyes with his own and whispered, "Because I think your mommy was murdered, Penny."

3

THE RED-AND-BLACK CAR PULLED INTO THE PARKING AREA while Zach was making lunch. It carried a Massachusetts license plate, the first three digits of which were 750. He did not know at the time that the 750 digits were given to year-round residents of the island that year. Nor was there anything about the man who stepped from the car which could have identified him as a native. He was tall and blond, and he moved with lithe familiarity toward the house. Watching from the kitchen window, Zach saw the man glance at the Plymouth, rub a hand across his chin, and then start for the house.

He stopped just outside the kitchen door. He didn't knock. He put his face close to the mesh of the screen and said, "Hi."

"Hello," Zach answered.

"You Zach Blake?"

"Yes."

The man opened the screen door and stepped into the kitchen. "I'm Pete Rambley," he said.

The way Rambley walked into the house without being invited annoyed Zach. He looked more closely at the man. There was a trace of a smile on Rambley's mouth, a touch of sardonic humor in his blue eyes.

"What's on your mind?" Zach asked.

"Your rental."

"What about it?"

"Seems to be a little confusion down at the Dubrows. Shame Carol ain't here because she'd clear it up in a minute. Anne's got no head for business."

"No?"

"No." Rambley stared at him, the blue eyes still mildly amused. "I'm afraid we rented this house to somebody else, Mr. Blake."

"I'm afraid I heard this story before," Zach said.

"Mmm, well maybe you didn't listen too close the first time around."

Zach put down the skillet he was holding and turned from the stove. "Meaning?" he said.

"Meaning I think you'll have to get out, Mr. Blake."

Zach did not answer for a moment. Then he said, "Don't be ridiculous. I paid for this house and—"

"But you didn't, Mr. Blake."

"I wired $500 to Mrs. Dubrow yesterday morning. Even if they'd sent it by carrier pigeon, it'd have got here by now."

"We didn't get any money, Mr. Blake."

"Then call Western Union. It's probably been waiting there since—"

"I already did."

"I don't believe you," Zach said flatly.

Rambley shrugged. "Call them yourself. You got a phone here?"

"I don't have to call them," Zach said. "I *know* I sent the money. Suppose you just get out of my kitchen, Mr. Rambley."

Rambley planted his feet wide and clenched his fists, as if he were preparing for a battle. Then, calmly, he said, "I guess I'll have to get the police."

"I guess so," Zach said tightly.

"Nice meeting you, Mr. Blake," Rambley said, and he walked out of the house. Zach watched him start the car, back around, and drive up the road, a cloud of dust swelling up behind the vehicle. He waited until both dust and automobile had vanished. Then he went to the telephone and dialed the operator.

"Get me Western Union," he said.

He waited.

"Western Union," a voice said briskly.

"My name is Zachary Blake," he said. "I wired $500 from New York yesterday morning to Mrs. Carol Dubrow in Chilmark. Can you tell me whether or not that money was claimed?"

"Yesterday morning, sir?"

"Yes."

"One moment, please." Zach waited. The voice came back. "Yes, sir. Mrs. Dubrow collected on that wire late yesterday afternoon."

"Mrs. Dubrow herself?" Zach asked.

"I don't know her personally, sir," the woman said. "But whoever collected was required to show identification."

"Thank you," Zach said. He hung up and went to the back porch. Penny had already collected two dozen shells from the beach and was arranging them on the wooden desk like British infantrymen.

"Want some lunch, honey?" he asked.

"I'm starved," Penny said. "How do you like my army?"

"Little girls shouldn't think of armies," Zach said.

"Girls are braver than boys, didn't you know that, Dad?"

"I hope they're hungrier, too," he said. "Scrambled eggs coming up in five minutes. I've got to make a phone call first."

"Okay," Penny said, and she went back to arranging her shells.

He went through the house and into the pantry off the kitchen. The telephone rested on a shelf there. He drew a stool up to the shelf and then opened his wallet and took out the letter.

The letter had been mailed from the island four days previously. It had been sent by air, and had been addressed to him at Resignac Broadcasting in New York. He had not received it until yesterday morning. He had dialed information, and then placed a call immediately to the sender, a woman named Evelyn Cloud. Her voice on the telephone had bordered on the narrow edge of terror. She refused to discuss the letter. She refused to discuss Mary. She would not tell him anything except face to face. He told her he would come to the island instantly, and then he phoned Mrs. Dubrow and arranged for the rental of the Fielding house.

He had deliberately chosen the house he and Mary had shared the summer before. He had deliberately chosen it because Evelyn Cloud's letter had reopened a closed issue—and if there were any truth at all to her words, perhaps the Fielding house would serve as the logical base of operations.

He spread the letter open on the shelf and read it again. It had been written in a hurried, uncertain scrawl.

Gay Head, July 10

Dear Mr. Blake,

My conscience can not be still no longer.

Your wife Mary did not drown accident.

Evelyn Cloud

He read the words once more, and then again. And then he flipped over the letter to where he'd written the woman's number when he'd got it from Information in New York. Hastily, he dialed.

"Hello?" It was the voice of a young boy, and Zach felt momentary annoyance.

"May I please speak to Evelyn Cloud?" he said.

"Who's this?" the boy asked.

"Zachary Blake."

"What do you want?"

"I want Evelyn Cloud."

"That's my mother," the boy said. "Why do you want her?"

"Would you call her to the phone, please?"

"She's getting ready to go out on the boat."

"Well, get her before she leaves," Zach said.

"Just a second."

Zach waited. The pantry was small and hot. Impatiently, he drummed on the shelf.

"Hello?"

"Mrs. Cloud?"

"Yes."

"This is Zachary Blake."

"Who?"

"Zachary Blake."

"I don't know you, Mr. Blake," the woman said.

"You sent me a letter," Zach answered. "I spoke to you on the phone yesterday, remember?"

"I didn't send you no letter. I didn't talk to you."

"Mrs. Cloud, it's about my wife Mary. You said—"

"I don't know your wife Mary," the woman said.

"But you wrote me—"

"I don't know how to write," the woman said.

"What is it?" Zach asked. "What are you afraid of?"

"I ain't afraid of nothing. I don't know you, Mr. Blake."

"Can't you talk? Is someone there with you?"

"Just my son. I don't know you, Mr. Blake."

"Do you want money? Is that it?"

"I don't want nothing."

"I'm coming to Gay Head, Mrs. Cloud. Right now. I've got to—"

"Don't come. I'm going out on the boat. I won't be here."

"I'm coming."

"I don't know you, Mr. Blake. Good-by," she said, and she hung up.

"Mrs. Cloud, wait a—"

The line was dead. He hung up and tried the number again. He got a busy signal. Either Evelyn Cloud was talking to someone else, or she'd taken the receiver off the cradle. He slammed down the phone, looked up Cloud in the local directory, and found a listing for John Cloud in Gay Head.

He went out to the back porch then and said, "Come on, Penny."

Penny saw his eyes and did not question his sudden command. She scrambled to her feet, took his hand, and left her scattered shells on the porch.

4

IT WAS ALMOST IMPOSSIBLE, ZACH DISCOVERED, TO FIND a house on the island without specific directions concerning its location. He should have remembered that from the previous summer when invitations for cocktails were accompanied by the most elaborate back-road instructions.

He drove into Gay Head on the South Road, passing Turnaround Hill and the painters looking over their easels to the gray-shrouded view of Quitsa and Menemsha Ponds. He passed Clam Point Cove, and then the Gay Head town line, and then he began stopping at every mailbox on the highway. He could not find one for John Cloud.

When he reached the Gay Head lighthouse and the colored clay cliffs dropping to the sea at the end of the island, he didn't know where to go next. He parked the car and started up the steep incline to the cliffs. Penny held his hand tightly. Two old Indians were sitting behind their counters of souvenirs. One, a white-haired man wearing khaki trousers, a sports shirt, and a feather in a band around his head, smiled at Penny.

"Are you an Indian?" she asked.

"Yes," he said.

"A *real* Indian?"

"An Algonquin," the man said, smiling.

At the next counter, the second Indian sat with his arms folded across his chest. A sign Scotch-taped to the counter read:

YOU NO PAY 50¢
YOU NO TAKE PICTURE.

Zach took his chances with the first Indian.

"Good afternoon," he said.

The Indian smiled. "Souvenir of Gay Head, sir?" he asked.

"How much is the tomahawk?" Zach said.

"One dollar," the Indian answered.

"Do you want a tomahawk, Penny?"

"Is it a *real* tomahawk?" Penny asked.

"Made by Gay Head Indians," the man said.

"I'll take it," Zach said. He hefted the tomahawk from the counter. A heavy flat stone, gaily painted, served as its striking head. A piece of wood had been split to form a handle for the stone which was lashed tightly to the wood. "Don't hit anybody with that," Zach said, and he handed it to Penny and paid the Indian.

"Thank you, sir," the Indian said.

"I'm trying to locate somebody in Gay Head," Zach said. "How do I go about it?"

"Ask," the Indian said.

"Her name's Evelyn Cloud." The Indian nodded. "Do you know her?"

"Yes. She's an Indian."

"Where do I find her?" Zach asked.

"Go back the way you came," the man said. "You'll pass a yellow mailbox about a half-mile up the road. Take the next dirt road after that. John Cloud's house is at the end of that road." The Indian paused. "He may not be there now. He's a swordfisherman. It's calm today, good for swordfish. He may be out in the boat."

"I'm not looking for him. I'm looking for Evelyn Cloud."

The Indian shrugged. "She goes with him sometimes. Sometimes the boy goes, too. Little Johnny."

"Thank you," Zach said.

"Thank *you,* sir," the Indian answered.

At the next counter, the Indian with his no-pay sign looked at Zach stoically. Penny noticed the look and said, "Well, we haven't even got a camera, you know!"

She whipped her ponytail saucily, and then went down to the car.

They passed the yellow mailbox and turned off onto the next dirt road. The sand had rutted itself into two tracks on either side of a grass-and-rock mound which scraped at the low-slung bottom of the Plymouth. Driving slowly, certain the entrails of the car were being ripped out piece by piece, Zach continued up the hill. At last he saw a smear of gray showing through the pines and scrub oak. The smear lengthened into the gable of a house, and then the house itself as Zach wheeled around a curve and came into a clearing.

He pulled up the hand brake and opened the door on his side of the car. The gray gauze of the sky was tearing off to reveal patches of blue. It was going to be a nice day, after all.

"Can I come with you, Daddy?" Penny asked.

"All right," he said.

He waited for her to climb out of the car, and then they started up towards the house together. The front porch of the gray structure was covered with paint cans, brushes, and flat stones of varying sizes and shapes, each painted brightly with would-be Indian symbols and left on the porch to dry. Penny made the connection between the stones and the tomahawk in her hand instantly.

"Was it made here?" she asked.

"Probably," Zach said. He knocked on the screen door. There was no answer. "Mrs. Cloud," he called. He knocked again, and then tried the door. It was locked. "Do you have a nail file in your purse?" he asked Penny.

"I think so," she said. He waited while, womanlike, she dug into the contents of her small purse. She handed him the file in its blue leather case, and he stuck the narrow sliver of metal into the crack where door met jamb. Shoving upwards, he released the screen door hook from its eye, and opened the door.

"Mrs. Cloud!" he called.

"I don't think she's home," Penny said.

"Let's go in, anyway."

"That's impolite," Penny said.

"I know. And don't you ever do it." He took her hand and walked into the house. Something was on the stove cooking. He could not place the smell. It boiled furiously in a big aluminum pot. "Think she'd go out and leave something boiling on the stove?" he asked.

"Mommy never did," Penny said.

"No." He stood in the center of the kitchen and called, "Mrs. Cloud!" and his voice echoed through the stillness of the house. A door was closed at the opposite end of the kitchen. He started for the door with Penny at his heels. He opened the door, began walking into the other room, and then stopped abruptly.

"Stay where you are, Penny," he said.

"Why? What—?"

"Stay there!" he said, and his voice carried the unmistakable ring of parental command. Penny stopped dead in her tracks. Zach entered the room and closed the door behind him. A fly was caught against the screen door leading out to the back of the house, its buzz filling the living room.

A woman lay on the floor in the center of the room.

Her hair was black, and her skin was bronzed. She was no older than thirty-eight. The top of her skull had been brutally crushed so that the blood poured onto her forehead and down her face, streamed over her neck and stained the pale blue flowered house dress she wore. Her mouth was open in what must have been the trailing end of a scream. Her eyes, wide and brown, splashed with rampant blood, stared up at the ceiling of the room. There was terror in the lifeless eyes, a terror captured and then frozen by death.

He was suddenly covered with sweat.

He wiped the back of his hand across his mouth, and then he stared down at the dead woman, incapable of speech or movement, fighting the tight nausea in his stomach. With conscious effort, he clicked his mind shut like a hair-trigger trap, and the nausea vanished to be replaced by a violent, unreasoning anger.

The room came into sharp, clear focus.

There had been a struggle. A lamp had been knocked from one of the end tables, and a straight-backed chair had been overturned. A dish towel was on the floor next to the woman, so he surmised she had come into the living room from the kitchen, walking into an ambush. He went to the back door. The screen there was unlocked. Three steps led down to the sloping sand and then into the woods. He glanced through the screen briefly and then came back into the room.

The weapon rested some three feet behind the woman's shattered skull. Its stone head was smeared with blood, as was its wooden shaft. A souvenir tomahawk, a close twin to the one Penny held in her hand outside. He did not touch it. He stooped down close to it and looked at it, but he did not touch it. He saw the medallion then. It was a thin bronze circle, and he might have missed it had he not stooped to look at the tomahawk. He picked it up and studied it.

A link from a chain was still caught in the metal loop at the top of the medallion. Had the woman torn this from her attacker's throat? The medallion carried the raised stamping of a sailboat. Above the boat were the words THIRD PRIZE 1947 in a semicircle. Below the boat, forming another semicircle along the bottom edge of the medallion, were the words TAXTON CLUB REGATTA, MIAMI. Zach put the medallion in his pocket and then stooped close to the woman again.

Her right hand was clutched tightly. He lifted it. It was still warm. She could not have been dead very long. Clutched in the hand were a number of long blond hairs. Even if he had not seen the torn roots he'd have automatically surmised the hairs had been ripped from her attacker's scalp. A silver signet ring on the woman's hand caught his eye. He turned her fist gently, looked at the ring, and felt sudden despair and hopelessness.

He had known it all along, he supposed, from the moment he'd opened the door on the woman's body, had known all along who she was, and that death had sealed her mouth and rendered meaningless the words in her letter. But the ring corroborated the knowledge, presented a plain and inescapable fact from which there was no retreat.

The initials on the ring were *E.C.*

The dead woman on the living-room floor was Evelyn Cloud.

Gently, he lowered her hand. He stood up. He supposed he had known all along, too, that he would not report this to the police. He certainly would not have pocketed the medallion if he'd intended calling the police. He knew instinctively that involvement in a homicide would keep him from accomplishing what he'd come here to do. He could not waste time clearing himself with the police. And he also knew instinctively that the death of Evelyn Cloud was inextricably connected with the drowning of Mary. And so he turned his back on the body, wiped the inside knob of the living-room door with his handkerchief, opened the door with the cloth covering his fingers, closed it, and wiped the outside knob.

"What are you doing?" Penny asked.

"Shhh," he said. "Did you touch anything in here?"

"No. Is someone dead?"

He looked at her, surprised for a moment, and then remembered the educational facilities of television. "Yes," he said. "Someone's dead."

Penny nodded. "Who?"

"The woman we came to see. Let's get out of here."

He opened the screen door, let Penny out, and then wiped the knob clean. As they drove out to the main road, he wondered if his tires would leave tracks in the packed sand.

5

THE BLONDE WAS WAITING AT THE HOUSE.

She sat on the front steps smoking a cigarette. She wore a full skirt and a halter, and her legs were crossed casually, too casually. She looked up as the Plymouth approached, but she did not uncross her legs, nor did she seem conscious of what the wind was doing to her skirt. She continued smoking leisurely, her eyes never leaving Zach as he stepped out of the car and went around to the other side for Penny. Then she dropped her cigarette to the sand and extended one sandaled foot to put it out, the wind catching at her skirt, billowing it upwards so that a long length of smooth golden thigh was revealed.

"Hi," she said. Her voice was huskily rich. "I've been waiting for you."

Zach and Penny came over to where she was sitting. "Have you?" he said.

"You *are* Zachary Blake, aren't you?" She smiled. Her face was very tanned, and her smile was wide and white. Her eyes were an intense blue against the tan. There were tiny laughter wrinkles at the edges of her eyes. He combined the voice and the face and the mature body and came up with an age of thirty-four or so.

"I'm Zachary Blake," he said. "Have you come to dispossess me?"

"What?" She looked up at him with honest puzzlement.

"Never mind. What can I do for you, Miss—?"

"Murphy. Enid Murphy. They used to call me 'Bridey' at cocktail parties, but it doesn't get a laugh any more."

"How do you do?" Zach said politely. "This is my daughter, Penny."

"Hello," Penny said.

"Hi," Enid answered.

"You still haven't told me."

"I'm from the *Vineyard Gazette,*" Enid said. "That's the local newspaper. And I'm not really *from* it. I contribute an occasional piece to it during the summer."

"So?"

"So I try to get to any celebrities before the mainland papers do."

"So?"

"So you're a celebrity."

"I am?"

"Indeed."

"That's news to me," Zach said.

"It shouldn't be. We get Resignac in Massachusetts, too, you know. Hordes of people up here begin their evening meals to the honeyed tones of Zachary Blake."

"You sound as if you don't like my broadcast," Zach said.

"I never listen to it," Enid admitted. "Shall I go stand in a corner?"

"Are you a native of the island?" he asked.

"No. I'm from Boston."

"And down for the summer?"

"And down for the summer," she repeated.

"What do you do when you're not tracking celebrities?"

"Swim. And sun. And drink."

"I meant in Boston."

"I'm a free-lance writer. I do articles for the women's magazines."

"That's entirely plausible," Zach said.

"You sound as if you don't like women's magazines."

"I never read them," Zach admitted. "Shall I go stand in a corner?"

Enid smiled. "*Touché.* Do I get the interview?"

"Will they pay you for it?"

"Sure."

"Come on in. I'll give you an interview and a drink. I hate to deprive any working stiff."

They started into the house and Penny said, "May I go down to the beach, Dad?"

"Not swimming."

"No. Just to get some shells."

"Sure," he said.

"May I take my tomahawk?"

"Sure."

"Thanks, Dad." She kissed him and then turned to Enid. "Nice meeting you, Miss Murphy," she said, and ran through the house and onto the back porch and then down the steps to the beach.

"She's adorable," Enid said.

"Thank you."

"Is your wife with you?"

"She's dead," Zach said simply.

"Oh, I'm sorry."

The room was silent for a moment. "What would you like to drink?" Zach asked. "I've only got rye."

"I'll have rye," Enid said. "On the rocks, please."

She stayed with him while he fixed the drinks. "Let me see," she said, taking out her pad and pencil. "Brown hair, brown eyes, strong jaw. I guess I can say 'the handsome Zachary Blake.' All right?"

Zack shrugged.

"How tall are you, Mr. Blake?"

"Five eleven and a half."

"We'll make it an even six. It sounds more romantic."

"Is this going into one of the women's magazines or just the local paper?"

Enid laughed. The laugh was rich and full, and for a moment it reminded him of other laughter, past laughter, and he forced the memory aside.

"How old are you, Mr. Blake?"

"Thirty-six," he said.

"I'm thirty-three," she answered. "Where were you born?"

"The Bronx."

"Boston meets the Bronx," she said, and she stopped writing and looked at him studiously. Her look embarrassed him somewhat. He handed her the drink.

"Why don't we go out on the porch?" he said. "It'll be more comfortable there."

"All right."

They sat facing the ocean. The steps from the house descended sharply into the shrubbery so that the beach was invisible from the porch. But they could hear the distant sound of the breakers, and the steady *dong-gong* of the bell buoy and the wild shrieking of the gulls overhead.

"That's the Gay Head light out there," Enid said.

"Um," Zach answered.

"Did you hear about the Indian woman?"

He felt instantly tense. He forced himself to relax. "Which Indian woman?"

"The one who was selling authentic Gay Head souvenirs made in Brooklyn?"

"Oh. Oh, no." He wiped his lip and then hastily gulped at his rye.

"I thought it was funny," Enid said, and she shrugged. "How long have you been in broadcasting, Mr. Blake?"

"Twelve years."

"Is there any truth to the rumor that you were supposed to take over the Ed Liggett show last year?"

"Yes, that's true."

"What happened?"

"My wife died," Zach said. "I didn't want the show any more."

They were silent again. Enid sipped at her drink.

"How'd she die?"

"Is this for your paper?" Zach asked.

"No. It's for me. Unless you'd rather not talk about it."

"She drowned," Zach said.

"Where?"

He gestured toward the water with his head. "Right out there."

"Were you with her?"

"No. I was here at the house. I was taping a farewell broadcast at Resignac's request. I was supposed to take over the Liggett show when I returned. Resignac thought it would be a good idea to do a farewell show instead of a news summary on the night I left radio. I was working on it when Mary . . . when my wife drowned."

"And you came back this summer?" Enid asked.

"Yes."

"Why?"

He did not answer.

"You get over it," Enid said suddenly.

"What? What did you say?"

"I said you get over it. My husband was a naval pilot. He was shot down over Okinawa. We'd been married two years." She paused and then sipped at her drink. "It takes a long while. But you get over it. You can't go on living in the past, Mr. Blake."

"Thanks," he said.

"I'm sorry if I was too frank."

"You weren't."

"Is the interview ended?"

"Not unless you've run out of questions."

"I have one more."

"Go ahead."

Enid Murphy put down her drink. "What are you doing tonight, Mr. Blake?"

He studied her for a moment and then said, "You sound like the Merry Widow."

"Do I?"

"Yes."

"That's not kind, Mr. Blake. Forget I asked." She rose and started for the screen door. "Thank you for the interview. I'll send you tear sheets."

He came up out of his chair quickly. "Wait!" he said, and he put out his hand involuntarily, and then drew it back. Enid stood just outside the screen door. Her blue eyes were very serious now. The wind flattened her skirt against her thighs, and she held it pinned there with her small black pad in one hand.

"Yes?"

"I'm sorry I was rude," he said. "I'm not doing anything tonight." He suddenly felt that he was being unfaithful to a memory, unfaithful to his reason for being here. But there was contained hurt in the woman's eyes, and somehow he did not wish to hurt her further.

"I'm having a small party at my house," she said. "Some of the people who are down for the regatta day after tomorrow. I thought you might like to come."

"What about Penny?" he asked.

"You can get a baby-sitter."

"I haven't used a baby-sitter in the past year," he answered.

"Maybe this is a good time to start," Enid said.

He nodded. "Maybe it is."

"There are signs outside the Menemsha store. Dozens of baby-sitters. Will you get one?"

"Yes," he said. "I'll get one."

Enid smiled. "I'll see you later then. Nine o'clock?"

"Yes."

"It's the house opposite the Coast Guard station. The one with the green shutters. Back of The Home Port."

"I'll find it."

"Good. It was nice meeting you, Bronx."

"It was nice meeting you, Boston," he said, and he was surprised to find himself smiling. He walked her to her car, and then went out onto the porch to wait for Penny. She did not return from the beach for a half-hour.

"I lost my tomahawk," she said. She came up the steps with her hands full of shells and rocks.

"Where?" he said.

"In the sand someplace. I put it down while I was hunting shells. Did you ever see a red-white-and-blue rock?"

"No."

"I've got one," she said, and she dumped the collection at her feet, and began picking through it. "See?"

"It's red-white-and-blue, all right. A very patriotic rock."

"Yes. I'm going to call it the George Washington Rock."

"That sounds like a popular song."

Penny laughed delightedly.

"Honey," he said.

"Yes?"

"Would you mind staying with a baby-sitter tonight?"

"Nope. Are you going out?"

"Yes."

"With Miss Murphy?"

"To her house, yes. For a party."

"That's good," Penny said. She nodded, as if in agreement with some hidden theory of her own.

"We've got a few things to do first, though," he said.

"Like what?"

"First we've got to get the baby-sitter, right?"

"Right."

"And next, I want to be at the dock when the swordfishing fleet comes in."

"Yes?"

"And then I'll buy you a lobster dinner at The Home Port. How about it?"

"Sometimes I love you, you know?" she said, and she threw her arms around his neck and kissed him.

6

JOHN CLOUD WAS SIX FEET FOUR INCHES TALL WITH THE shoulders and hips of a fullback. His head was massively compact, chiseled from brownstone. His eyes were squinting black in the uneven features of his face. He wore dungaree trousers, a denim shirt and a white canvas jacket. His head was bare, and his hair was as black as gunpowder.

He leaped from the boat to the dock and then pulled his son ashore after him. He moved with muscular nonchalance. It was not difficult to picture John Cloud stalking a deer through the woods, wearing only a breech clout and carrying a bow and arrow.

Zach stood at the end of the dock, Penny's hand in his own. A sharp wind blew off the water, and he was happy he'd insisted on her wearing a sweater. They had gone into the general store and post office, the thriving center of Menemsha summer activity. He had asked the woman behind the counter to recommend a sitter from the score or more of those whose advertising signs were tacked to the outside of the store. The woman had suggested a girl named Thelo Ford, and Zach had called her from the pay phone outside the store. Miss Ford promised to be at the Fielding house at 8:45 sharp. Yes, she knew where it was. No, he needn't pick her up; her mother would drop her off. Satisfied, he had bought Penny a half-dozen Golden Books and then gone to wait on the dock.

The wind had torn patches in the gray overcast, and the patches had expanded until they formed a clear stretch of blue over the water. The blue was painful to the eyes, a sharp, unrelieved, glaring blue that gained intensity from the darkness of the water. Along the dock, the pleasure boats bobbed idly. Tied to stout poles, the tails of previous swordfish catches rose to the sky, the wide wings black against the piercing blue. From a yacht at the end of the dock, Zach could hear the drunken laughter of an afternoon cocktail party.

And then he saw the tall Indian and the small boy, and he instantly knew this was John Cloud and his son. He waited until the man approached, and then he said, "Mr. Cloud?"

Cloud broke his stride. The black eyes flicked to Zach's face. There was, for the fleeting of an instant, fear in the eyes.

"Yes?"

"Are you John Cloud?"

"Yes?" The "yes" was still a question. The fear had vanished from the eyes to be replaced by caution.

"My name's Zachary Blake."

"Yes?"

"I received a letter from your wife."

"My wife's business is her own," Cloud said, and he began walking again. Zach caught up with him.

"Just a minute, Cloud," he said.

"What do you want?"

"I talked to your wife from New York yesterday."

"I don't know about it." Cloud glanced over his shoulder. The fear had seeped back into his eyes.

"Mr. Cloud, my wife drowned here last year. She—"

"I don't know about it," Cloud repeated.

"Your *wife* knew about it!"

"Her business is her business. She's a foolish woman. Her tongue—"

"Mr. Cloud, don't turn away from me, please!"

Their eyes met. A tic had started at the side of Cloud's mouth. Again, he glanced over his shoulder. Then, in a whisper, he said, "Go back to New York, Mr. Blake. I can't help you. I've got a wife and a young boy. Don't bother me, Mr. Blake. I don't want trouble. Go back to New York."

"You've got a stake in this," Zach said.

"Have I?" Cloud said, and he turned away.

"Your wife is dead," Zach said.

He could not have stopped the man more effectively had he struck him with a baseball bat. Cloud drew up short, the words slamming into his eyes and face. His brow lowered menacingly.

"What do you mean?"

"She's dead."

"Where?"

"Your house."

"How do you know?"

"I saw her."

Cloud was silent for a moment. Then he muttered. "Those rotten bastards," and he took Johnny's hand.

"Will you help me now?"

"I've got a son," Cloud said. "I've still got a son. Get out of my way, Mr. Blake."

"Who killed her, Cloud?"

"Get out of my way!"

He swung his arm sidewards, flinging Zach out of his path. Zach staggered backwards, almost losing his balance. He fell against a dock pile, shoved himself erect and yelled, "Cloud! Goddamnit, wait a minute!"

Cloud did not answer. He strode off the dock, clutching his son's hand tightly. He opened the door of an old Chevrolet, deposited his son on the seat and then climbed in and slammed the door. He started the car immediately and pulled away in a screech of dust and burning rubber.

Zach stared after the retreating cloud of dust. He took Penny's hand. Disconsolately he said, "We'd better get dinner."

7

THE SITTER ARRIVED AT 8:45 ON THE BUTTON. SHE WAS sixteen, a brunette with large brown eyes and a mouth that was too wide. She wore no lipstick. She wore chino trousers and a gray sweatshirt. She looked like a physical education major at a women's college. She looked as if she might wrestle alligators during the baby-sitter off-season.

He began showing her through the house, and the first thing she said was, "I don't like Elvis Presley."

"Don't you?"

"No. That surprises you, doesn't it?"

"It certainly does surprise me," Zach said.

"All teenagers are supposed to like Elvis Presley. Well, I don't. I don't believe in conformity. Teenagers are the biggest conformists around."

"I suppose so," Zach said. "This is Penny's bedroom. If it starts to rain, or it gets too breezy, close the window, will you?"

"Sure. My full name is Thelonious Ford, did you know that?"

"No, I didn't."

"Sure. My parents named me after Thelonious Sphere Monk. He's a jazz musician."

"I see."

"My brother's name is Krupa Ford. You know Gene Krupa, of course?"

"Of course."

"My parents dig jazz," Thelo said. "That's how come we got the names."

"That's very interesting," Zach said. He had looked up Enid Murphy's phone number before dinner. She was one of the summer residents who, by making a small payment to the telephone company, had had her name listed in the local directory. He gave Thelo the number now and said, "If there's any trouble at all, call me at this number."

"Don't worry," Thelo said. "I'm an experienced sitter."

"I know. But if anything should give you trouble—"

"What could give me trouble?"

"I don't know. But I'll be at this number, just in case."

"Sure. Come on, Penny," Thelo said, "I'll read you a story."

Zach kissed Penny and said, "Nine-thirty, all right, honey?"

"Okay," she said. "Have a good time," and she scrambled onto Thelo's ample lap.

The party was in full swing when he got there. He pulled up near the Coast Guard station, and then walked slowly toward the house. Outside, he lighted a cigarette. He felt suddenly strange, and nervous, and curiously awkward. He had avoided all social engagements since Mary's death a year ago. He had become a literal hermit, going nowhere except with Penny. And now he was going to a party. Alone. Without Mary. He stood just outside the white fence, half-tempted to leave. The sky was black overhead, buckshot peppered with silver stars. He could hear the ocean, and the ever-present shrieking of the gulls holding their convention out on Gull Island. He could remember what Mary had said about the early morning chatter of the gulls last year. "They're discussing a book called *Should Birds Hold Executive Positions?*" He smiled grimly. The coal of his cigarette burned in the darkness. There was party laughter inside the house. Someone began playing a piano, and suddenly he wanted no part of it, wanted to get back quickly and unobserved, wanted to get back to his daughter and his memories of a woman who had filled his life. He squashed out the cigarette and took a step away from the picket fence.

"Zach?" the voice said.

He stopped.

"Aren't you coming in?"

He turned. Enid Murphy stood just outside the screened porch. The subdued light from the house caught at her blond hair. She wore a black blouse with a scoop throat. A turquoise-colored skirt flared out over her hips. The belt at her waist was made of linked silver. There were silver earrings on her ears, each dotted with a tiny turquoise stone. She moved out of the light and the blond hair lost its reflection. The blond hair . . .

And then he remembered that the hairs clenched in the fist of the dead Evelyn Cloud were blond, and he wondered abruptly if Enid Murphy had really wanted an interview that afternoon.

"Yes," he said. "I'm coming in."

She took his hand, squeezed it briefly, and said, "I'm glad you could come, Zach," and then she led him into the house.

The crowd was an arty one. Remembering the Menemsha parties from last year, he had not expected less. A cameraman who had worked with the Japanese on *Gate of Hell* was discussing the superiority of their color photography. A bearded poet was complaining to a Broadway producer about the cultural decline of the American reading public as demonstrated by the sales of his latest poetry volume. The piano player was playing "The Boulevard of Broken Dreams" and the author of a best-selling novel about big business was singing in a mock French accent. Someone put a drink into Zach's hand, and he watched the dance director for one of television's big comedy hours throw back her skirt and point her toe at the ceiling in time to the piano music. In deference to propriety, she was wearing a black leotard under the skirt.

Zach sipped at his drink.

"What do you do?" the poet asked him.

"I'm a radio announcer."

"Yeah?"

"Yeah."

"A disc jockey?"

"No."

"What then? Station breaks?"

"No," Zach said. "I'm a news commentator."

"It's news that destroys the culture of America," the poet said. "Why don't you grow a beard?"

"Why should I?"

"Why the hell shouldn't you? You're a man, aren't you?"

"Sure."

"What brings you to the Vineyard?"

"Fun," Zach answered. "Hilarity."

"You sound cynical as hell. You're probably one of the bastards destroying culture in America."

"It's my hobby," Zach said. "Excuse me. I need a refill." He shoved his way through the crowd, walking toward the makeshift bar which had been set up in the kitchen. A man wearing sneakers, Navy grays, and an Italian sports shirt unbuttoned to his navel was mixing a stiff gin and tonic.

"Greetings," the man said. "I'm Freddie."

"I'm Zach."

"Crummy party, isn't it?" Freddie said.

"Not bad. Par for the course," Zach said.

Freddie looked at him with interested blue eyes. His face bore the dissipated ingrained appearance of too much money and too much whisky.

"Zach what?" Freddie said.

"Blake."

"Never heard of you."

"I never heard of you, either."

"Freddie Barton," he said, almost viciously. "My father owns half the movie theaters in New York State."

"Who owns the other half?" Zach asked. He poured rye over some ice, and then edged away from the table, planning on the shortest escape route.

"My uncle," Freddie said, and he laughed. "You here for the regatta?"

"No." Zach moved back to the table. "Are you?"

"Yes," Freddie said, and Zach's eyes moved upward on the man's face and stopped at the blond hair worn in a high crown off the forehead.

"Do you sail a lot?" Zach asked.

"I do. I've got a Raven. It's a small boat, but it'll beat any damned craft on the water. I know. I've got cups to prove it."

"Medals, too?"

"A few. Why? Don't you believe me?"

"I believe you," Zach said. "Ever race in Miami?"

"I've raced everywhere."

"The Taxton Club?"

"Second rate," Freddie said. "Did you race there?"

"No."

"Then what made you think of it?"

"I just thought of it."

"Mmm," Freddie said. He studied Zach again. "You're beginning to bore me, Blake."

The girl with the black leotard under her skirt came into the kitchen. "Enid told me to dance with the handsome stranger," she said. "Which one of you is the handsome stranger?"

"It must be Freddie," Zach said. "His father owns half the movie theaters in New York State," and he walked out of the room. He found Enid talking to a woman doctor who'd just come back from the Russian zone of Germany. She waited for a break in the conversation before looking up.

"Didn't Marcia find you?" she asked.

"She found me," Zach said. "But somehow we lost each other again."

"Dr. Reutermann, I'd like you to meet Zachary Blake," Enid said. "Zach, Inge Reutermann."

Zach shook hands with the woman. Her grip was firm and strong. She had the square-shaped hands of a man, and the brown eyes behind the tortoise-shell glasses were shrewdly intelligent.

"You are the news commentator, is that so?" she said. She spoke English precisely, biting her words with Teutonic meticulousness.

"Yes, I am."

"Do you comment, actually, or just report?"

"I comment," Zach said.

"I could tell you things about the Russian zone."

"I'd love to hear them," Zach said.

"Not now," Enid interrupted. "I want to dance with you, Zach."

"I—"

"Please?" she said.

"Certainly. Excuse us, Dr. Reutermann."

"Inge," the doctor corrected, smiling.

The piano player was playing "Smoke Gets in Your Eyes." A busty girl in sweater and shorts was singing to it in a high soprano. Out on the screened porch, three couples were dancing.

"That's one of my favorite songs," Enid said. "But how she's murdering it!"

"I *used* to like it, too," Zach said with a grin.

"How do you like the crew?"

She was in his arms now, quite close to him. He could smell the faint trace of perfume in her hair. Her cheek against his was smooth and vibrant.

"They're people," he said.

"Is that the best you can say for them?"

"That's the best you can say for anybody," Zach said.

"And the hostess?"

"The hostess is nice." He paused. "Tell me about Freddie Barton."

"A spoiled brat, rich as New Jersey soil. Why?"

"Does he sail a lot?"

"It's his life. He's married to that goddamned Raven. I think he goes to be with the spinnaker."

"Ever see him wearing a small medallion around his neck?"

Enid looked at him curiously. "My, you certainly make fascinating dance conversation," she said.

"Have you?"

"A medallion? Around his neck? Why, I don't know. I never noticed. Are you serious?"

"Just wondering," Zach said. "Is the regatta held every year at this time?"

"In July sometimes, yes."

"Was Freddie Barton here for last year's regatta?"

"I think so."

"Would you know when the regatta took place last year?"

"No, but I can find out. I'm sure the *Gazette* has a morgue. Do you want me to look it up for you?"

"Yes, would you?"

"First thing in the morning. I don't understand, Zach."

"I don't, either. Not yet, anyway."

She moved closer into his arms. "Have you seen the Murphy view yet?" she asked.

"No. What is the Murphy view?"

"Come." She moved out of his arms, took his hand and led him outside. The garden was very still and very black. The Gay Head light blinked red and then white. The light far off at the end of the jetty reflected in the water. Out on the ocean there were more lights, the lights of boats soundlessly cruising.

"That's the Murphy view," she said.

"It's nice."

And suddenly she moved against him and brought her arms up about his neck. Her mouth caught his, held it in a warm kiss. Her lips were full and longing. Her mouth was vibrantly alive, and he could smell the perfume in her hair, and then she drew away from him.

"That's the Murphy kiss," she said.

"Yes." He reached for his handkerchief and wiped the lipstick from his mouth.

"Was it very painful?"

"No."

"Zach—"

"Shouldn't we go inside?" he asked.

She stared at him for a moment and then thrust out her lower lip in a completely girlish gesture. "Sure. Sure, let's go inside."

She deposited him with Dr. Reutermann, and went to get herself a drink. He watched her as she crossed the room. The bearded poet stopped her with a complaint about the whisky. Apparently it, too, was destroying the cultural potential of America.

"Is it true, Mr. Blake?" the doctor said.

"If it's Inge, then it's Zach," he replied.

"Zach, forgive me. Is it true?"

"Is what true?"

"That the government is putting a Nike launching site on Martha's Vineyard?"

"I don't know," he said.

"It would be interesting, don't you think?"

"I . . . I suppose so," he said. He stared at the woman with renewed interest.

"Don't look at me that way, Zach," she said, chuckling. "I'm not a Russian spy. I was only in the Russian zone for two days to give my learned opinion on a cardiac case. I'm a heart specialist, you know."

"I didn't know."

"Yes. But I must admit the notion of a Nike site here on the sand dunes has great melodramatic possibilities. Don't you think so?"

"Yes," he said, and he wondered suddenly how long plans for the site had been in progress. As long ago as last summer?

"I must tell it to that novelist fellow. What was his book?"

"The Pirate's Gold," Zach said absently.

"It is a sea story?"

"No. It's about big business."

"He is famous in this country?"

"Yes," Zach said.

"He is not famous in Germany," Dr. Reutermann said flatly. "But he will think it farfetched. I cannot conceive of a spy story set on this beautiful island, can you?"

"I don't know," Zach said.

"But then, there is violence everywhere, is there not? That Indian woman today."

He felt a sudden warning rocket into his brain. Casually, he lighted a cigarette. "What Indian woman?"

"Have you not heard? Someone murdered an Indian woman at Gay Head. The police are investigating it now. It was on the radio, *ja*. This evening. You did not hear about it?"

"No," Zach said.

He could hear a telephone ringing insistently somewhere in the house. The piano player stopped his rendition of "I'll Walk Alone" long enough to yell "Telephone!" and then began playing "I'll Never Smile Again," almost as if he thought he were playing the same song.

This is nostalgia night, Zach thought. This is old-song, and beach-view, and a-kiss-from-a-blonde night. This is hold-the-torch-high night. This is memory-of-Mary night, full blown, sitting on my heart like a black stone. This is Freddie and his regattas, and Inge Reutermann and her Nike launching sites, and this is a night to wonder why my wife was killed, and a night to jump in fear whenever a dead Indian woman is mentioned. This is a night of confusion and memory, and I'm lost, good God, I'm lost in the wilderness!

"Zach!"

He looked up sharply. Enid was calling him. "Yes?"

"It's for you."

"What?"

"The phone."

"Oh. Excuse me, Inge." He threaded his way through the crowd, and Enid led him to a bedroom off the corridor. The phone was resting on a night table near the bed.

"The sitter?" he asked, picking up the receiver.

"Not unless the sitter is a man," Enid said. She stood in the doorway watching him. He sat on the edge of the bed and brought the receiver to his mouth.

"Hello?" he said.

"Blake?" The voice was muffled and unclear. It sounded as if it were coming from a long way off.

"Yes?"

"Get out of that house and get off the Vineyard," the voice said.

"Wh—?"

"Get out! Unless you want what Evelyn Cloud got. Do you hear me, Blake? Get out!"

"Who is—?"

The line went dead. He sat staring at the receiver for a moment, and then suddenly he thought of Penny alone with a baby-sitter in a house on the edge of the ocean. He slammed the receiver into its cradle and leaped to his feet.

"What is it?" Enid asked.

"I've got to get home," he said. "Thanks for the party."

"And the kiss?"

"That, too. Thanks for everything."

"Will I see you again, Zach?"

"Yes. I don't know. Look, I've got to get home."

"I'll come with you."

"How'll you get back?"'

"Someone'll pick me up. Or I'll walk. I don't care."

"What do you want, Enid?" he asked.

"I'm not sure yet," she said. "Right now, I want to go with you."

"Suit yourself," he said. "Come on."

In the living room, the piano player was playing "Talk of the Town."

8

THE HOUSE LIGHTS WERE OUT.

He felt his heart lurch when he saw the total darkness of the house, and he began cursing himself for leaving Penny alone with a sixteen-year old jazz fiend. He thumbed open the glove compartment, seized a flashlight, and ran out of the car to the kitchen door.

"Penny!" he shouted.

He slammed into the house and turned on the kitchen light, and then he went into the living room.

Thelonious Ford was unconscious on the floor.

He did not stop beside her. He ran instantly to Penny's bedroom and snapped on the light. The bed covers were thrown back. The bed was empty.

"Penny," he called, and then he heard footsteps behind him, and he whirled, bringing up the flashlight, ready to use it as a club.

"My God!" Enid said. "What—"

He pushed past her and went into the other bedroom. He ran upstairs, checking each room, checking the bathroom, even checking the closets. The house was empty. And then, the phone downstairs began ringing, the two signals that indicated his number on the party line. He went down the steps at a gallop and then into the pantry. He pulled the phone off its cradle.

"Hello," he said.

"She's gone, Blake," the voice said.

"Who is this? What have you—?"

"Shut up!"

Zach closed his mouth. He was squeezing the receiver tightly, as if trying to drain it of information.

"Shut up and listen," the voice said. "Your daughter's all right. She'll continue to be all right until tomorrow afternoon. There's a ferry leaving Vineyard Haven at 1:45 P.M., Blake. Have you got that? 1:45 P.M."

"I've got it."

"Good. You'd better be on that ferry. When you get off at Woods Hole, drive straight to Providence. You should be there by five o'clock, even if the traffic is heavy."

"Yes, but my daughter—"

"I said shut up!"

He was trembling, but he closed his mouth and waited. The man on the other end was silent for a moment.

"You ready to listen, Blake?"

"Yes."

"There's a restaurant in Providence called The Blue Viking. Your daughter will be waiting there for you at five o'clock. When you pick her up, go straight back to New York. Forget Martha's Vineyard, and don't ever come back. Have you got that, Blake?"

"The Blue Viking at five o'clock. Penny will be there."

"You've got it."

"How do I know she's all right now? Let me talk to her."

"Forget it, Blake. Just take me word for it. She's all right. Get on that 1:45 ferry tomorrow and drive like hell. And don't come back. Someone'll be watching at Vineyard Haven to make sure you board the boat. If he doesn't see you, your daughter—"

"I'll be on the boat," Zach said.

"Good. One last thing. Don't tell the police. Either now or later. If we hear even a hint that there's been a kidnaping—"

"I won't tell the police," he said quickly.

"Have you got it all?"

"Yes."

"Good. Have a nice trip home," the man said, and he hung up.

Zach signaled for the operator immediately.

"Yes, sir?"

"Operator, can you trace that call I was just speaking . . . that party I was just speaking to? Can you trace the call?"

"I'm sorry, sir. We are unable to do that."

"This is important!"

"I'm sorry, sir, but we're unable to—"

"Oh, never mind!" He slammed down the phone. Enid was waiting in the pantry doorway.

"What is it?" he said.

"Someone's kidnaped my daughter."

"What? For God's sake, Zach, call the police!"

"I can't. No." He thought for a moment. "They must be somewhere near. That phone call came right after we turned on the house lights. Thy must be able to see the house from wherever they are. One of the houses on the hill, maybe."

"Or a boat," Enid said.

"How could they have phoned from a boat?"

"They wouldn't have to. They could have signaled ashore as soon as they saw the lights go on. Someone anywhere along the coast could have made the call."

He stared at her suspiciously. "You seem to know a hell of a lot about it," he said.

"I'm only—"

"Are you in this, Enid?"

"In what? Do you mean—?"

"Everything."

"I'm not in anything," she said flatly.

"I hope you're not, Enid. But it was you who invited me to a party, you who suggested I leave Penny with a baby-sitter. If you're—"

"What do you take me for, Zach?"

"If you're mixed up in this—"

"You can't be serious!"

He stared at her and then sighed heavily. "Forgive me, I'm—" He shook his head. "Let's take a look at the sitter."

Thelo Ford was gaining consciousness when they went back into the living room. She sat up, saw Zach, and was ready to scream until he laid a comforting hand on her arm.

"What happened, Thelo?" he asked.

"I don't know. Someone knocked at the door, and I asked who it was. I wouldn't open the door until I knew who it was. 'It's me. Mr. Blake,' he said. So I opened it. And then somebody hit me, and that's all I remember. Was it a burglar? Is Penny all right?"

"Penny's fine," he lied, and Enid looked at him curiously. "Come on, I'd better take you home."

He dropped Thelo off first, and then he took Enid back to the party.

"I'm sorry," he said to her. "I shouldn't have snapped at you."

"What are you going to do, Zach?"

"Follow their instructions."

"Won't you call the police?"

"I can't. They'd—" He shook his head. "I can't."

"What are their instructions?"

"They want me off the island by 1:45 tomorrow. They'll be watching. I'll have to . . . Enid, I don't feel like talking. I'm sorry, but I can't seem to think straight. I want to get home. God, if they touch her—"

"She'll be all right. Don't worry." She squeezed his hand. "She'll be all right." She got out of the car and closed the door gently. "If you need help, Zach, anything, anything at all, call me. Just call," she said, and she started for the house. He sat watching her for a moment, and then turned his eyes from the house. He could see out over the water, could see the cruising lights of countless surface craft. Had one of those boats signaled ashore to someone waiting to make a call? Was Penny out on the water now, in one of those boats? He folded his arms on the steering wheel and then put his head down. He was suddenly very confused and very tired. He wanted his wife back, and he wanted his daughter back, and a wave of self-recrimination washed over him when he thought of Penny in the hands of strangers. If he had left well enough alone, if he had stayed in New York and thrown away Evelyn Cloud's letter, if he had only allowed dead ashes to settle, Penny would be safe now.

He started the car. Wearily, he drove through Menemsha.

The Massachusetts State Police were waiting for him back at the Fielding house.

He got out of the Plymouth, and a voice reached for him in the darkness.

"Mr. Blake?" A flashlight came up onto his face.

"Yes," he said, shielding his eyes.

"Just stay right where you are. We'll come to you."

He waited. The flashlight stayed on his face. He could hear the troopers' boots crunching in the packed sand. They stopped alongside him, the light still in his eyes.

"Can't you lower that flash?" he said.

"Sure." The light came down, spilling a cold glow onto the sand at their feet. "Mr. Blake, you'll have to come along with us."

"What for?" Zach asked.

"The lieutenant wants to talk to you."

"What about?"

"About a dead woman."

His eyes were getting accustomed to the darkness. He studied the trooper's solemn face and then said, "I don't know what you're talking about."

"A woman named Evelyn Cloud," the trooper said.

"I never heard of her."

"No? Mr. Blake, there's an old Indian at Gay Head. He sells souvenirs. He said a man and a little girl were asking about Evelyn Cloud this afternoon. He told them how to find her. He also sold the man a tomahawk, Mr. Blake."

The trooper paused. ''Evelyn Cloud was killed with a tomahawk, Mr. Blake. Want to come along with us now?''

''I bought that tomahawk for my daughter,'' Zach said.

''Where's your daughter now, Mr. Blake?''

''She's been . . .'' He stopped, suddenly remembering the warning voice on the telephone. *Don't tell the police.* ''She's . . . she's been sent home,'' he said. ''I sent her home. To her grandmother.''

''And I suppose she took that tomahawk with her, huh?''

''No, she lost it on the beach this aft . . .'' He let the sentence trail. It sounded ridiculous, it sounded absurd, it sounded like the flimsiest snap fabrication.

''That's very interesting, Mr. Blake,'' the trooper said drily. ''You can explain it all to the lieutenant. Come on now.''

He shrugged wearily, and followed them to their car.

9

IT WAS ONE O'CLOCK IN THE MORNING.

The state troopers had come all the way from Oak Bluffs, but they delivered Zach to the police in Edgartown. The Edgartown police were very polite and very friendly. The lieutenant from Axel Center across the Sound was very friendly and polite, too. But none of them could disguise the fact that they suspected Zach was implicated in a murder.

The lieutenant from Axel Center had come over on the ferry that afternoon after a call from the sheriff of Dukes County. He was a big man in his early forties with bright red hair and deep brown eyes. His voice was deep and patient, his manner cool but forceful. He wore a seersucker suit and a simply printed cotton tie. His shirt was an oddity which told Zach it was hand tailored; it had a button-down collar and French cuffs. The cuff links were two silver miniatures of a .38 automatic, one at each wrist. The real article hung in a barely concealed shoulder holster under the seersucker jacket.

"I'm Lieutenant Whitson," he told Zach. "Won't you sit down, Mr. Blake?"

Zach sat.

"It looks as if you may be in a little bit of trouble, Mr. Blake," Whitson said.

"It doesn't look that way to me," Zach answered.

Whitson smiled indulgently. "I can understand your annoyance, Mr. Blake," he said, "but there's nothing personal in this. If we can lift it off the personal plane, things'll be a lot easier for all of us. I'm sure you understand."

"I didn't kill that woman," Zach said.

"Well," Whitson said noncommittally. He paused, lighted a cigar, and then said, "Perhaps you don't mind answering a few questions?"

"I don't mind at all," Zach said.

"Very well. Were you at Gay Head with a blond girl of about nine or ten years old this afternoon?"

"I was."

"Did you buy a tomahawk from an Indian there?"

"I did."

"Where is that tomahawk now?"

"My daughter lost it at the beach. I'm sure we can find it when the sun comes up—if you're willing to take the trouble."

"We're willing to do anything that will establish your innocence, Mr. Blake."

"Sure," Zach said dispiritedly.

"Did you ask this Indian about Evelyn Cloud?"

"Yes."

"Why?"

"I wanted to see her."

"Why?"

"On a personal matter."

"The nature of which was what?"

"A personal matter," Zach insisted.

"Mr. Blake, you are not in the Army, and police investigation doesn't recognize the sanctity of a *personal* matter. Now perhaps you do not realize the seriousness—"

"I realize it,' Zach said. "If you don't mind, I'd like to call my lawyer."

"You can do that later," Whitson said. "Why'd you want to see this Cloud woman?"

"On a personal matter."

Whitson sighed heavily and blew out a cloud of smoke. "Mr. Blake," he said genially, "are you *trying* to make things tougher for yourself?"

"No, but—"

"What the hell are you trying to hide?" Whitson said. "Do you realize a murder's been committed?" There was something like shocked incredulity in his voice. "What the hell are you? A simpleton? This is *murder,* Mr. Blake. Murder! Now what do you have to say for yourself?"

"I didn't kill her."

"Did you go to her house this afternoon?"

Zach hesitated.

"Did you?"

"Yes."

"Did you talk to her?"

"No."

"Why not?"

"She was dead when I got there."

"I see." Whitson thought this over for a moment. "Why didn't you report her death to the police?"

"I didn't want to get involved."

"Well, you're involved now, mister," Whitson said, his voice turning suddenly brusque. "And you'd better start talking fast if you want to get *un*involved again."

"I want to call my lawyer," Zach said.

"There's no need to call your goddamn lawyer yet!" Whitson said angrily. "Wait until we book you, for God's sake! Play ball with us, Blake."

"I didn't kill her."

"Why'd you go there?"

"What difference does it make?"

"It may make a lot of difference. Right now, it looks as if you went there to kill her. Now did you or didn't you?"

"I didn't. I already told you she was dead when I—"

"That why *did* you go there?" Whitson shouted.

Zach was silent for a moment. He could not tell Whitson about the letter without elaborating on it further. And if the letter was responsible for Evelyn Cloud's death, wasn't Penny's kidnaping a further extension of the attempt to obliterate that letter and its ominous meaning? If he told Whitson about the letter, if he told him why he'd gone to see Evelyn Cloud, he would also have to tell him that Penny had been kidnaped. And if he did that, he would be endangering his daughter's life.

He sighed and said, "I want to call my lawyer."

"Okay," Whitson said, "have it your way. I didn't think you were a fool, Blake, but it shows how wrong a man can be." He shoved a phone across the desk. "Will this be a long-distance call?"

"Yes."

"Make it fast. This isn't the richest town in the world." He looked at his watch. "I'll give you five minutes," he said, and he went out of the room.

Zach picked up the phone and got the long-distance operator. He placed a person-to-person call to Sam Dietrich in New York, and then waited while the phone rang. His wrist watch read 1:35 A.M.

"Hullo?"

"Sam?"

"Mrmm?"

"Sam, are you awake?"

"Huh? Whossis?"

"This is Zach Blake."

"Oh, hi, Zach, whut . . ." There was a long pause. "It's 1:30 in the morning. What—?"

"I'm up at Martha's Vineyard, Sam. Are you awake?"

"I am, I am. What's the matter?"

"I'm in trouble with the police."

"What kind of trouble?"

"I'm being held on suspicion of murder."

"What! What did you say?"

"Suspicion of—"

"How the hell did you manage that?"

"Can you get up here, Sam?"

"Yeah, sure, sure. Where are you?"

"Edgartown."

"Jail?"

"Not yet. But I imagine I will be."

"The Edgartown jail. How do I get up there?"

"Northeast runs a flight up here. You can probably get a cab at the airport."

"Do they fly at night?"

"I don't know. You'll have to check."

"I'll check. If I'm not there tonight, it'll be first thing in the morning. You haven't admitted anything, have you?"

"No."

"You haven't made any statements?"

"No."

"Don't. What's the number there?" Zach gave it to him. "Okay, I'll check with the airlines, and I'll probably get back to you. Don't say another word until I get there." Sam paused. "Did you do it, Zach?"

"Hell, no."

"Okay, I'll see you," and he hung up.

Zach put the phone back onto the cradle. Whitson came into the room. "Finished?" he asked.

"Yes."

"You'll like the Edgartown jail," Whitson told him. "It's old, but very clean."

Zach didn't say anything. A uniformed Edgartown cop took his arm. In an attempt at humor, the cop asked, "Will you be staying for the regatta?"

From the street, you would never guess that the wooden building housed a jail. Only when you looked at the building from the side could you tell that the back half of it was made of brick. The front looked like a large private house complete with picket fence. A sign to the left of the doorway advised any approaching visitor that the sheriff of Dukes County kept offices in the building. Even the inside of the structure looked like the inside of someone's home.

Except for the cells.

The cells were at the back of the house in the brick half of the building. There were six cells downstairs and six cells upstairs. Each cell block contained three cells on opposite sides of the house. A heavy metal door closed off each cell block from the rest of the house. There was a small panel in each door, set at about eye level, with a metal flap which closed shut over it.

The Edgartown cop allowed Zach to walk between him and the jail keeper. They opened the metal door of the cell block on the left-hand side of the house, and then took him to a cell at the end of the hall. The brick inside the cell block was painted a peach yellow. The cells were large, at least ten by ten. There was a narrow cot in each of the three cells, and a metal cabinet recessed into the cell wall carried a metal bucket for sanitary purposes.

"If you have to go to the john," the keeper explained, "just yell. There's a real toilet at the end of the cell block." He opened the cell. "I'd offer you some magazines, but lights-out was hours ago."

"Thanks," Zach said.

"My advice is for you to get some sleep."

"That's good advice," Zach said.

The cell door clanged shut. The keeper and the cop left. At the far end of the cell block, the heavy metal door closed and then the lights went out again.

10

THE CALL FROM SAM DIETRICH CAME AT EIGHT IN THE morning. They led Zach from his cell and put him into a room with a desk and a phone. The receiver was already off the cradle. He picked it up and said, "Hello?"

"Zach?"

"Yes. Is that you, Sam?"

"Yeah. Listen, I—"

"Where are you?"

"In New York."

"When are you leaving?"

"That's just it. I'm not."

"What's the matter?"

"I can't get a damn plane reservation. It seems they're booked for weeks in advance. From Thursday to Monday. Apparently guys commute to that island as if they were going to Scarsdale. I told the airline it was an emergency, but the best they could do was put me on a waiting list."

"How about driving up, Sam?"

"I tried that, too. You've got to get a reservation in order to take a car onto the ferry. And they haven't got any space left this weekend."

"Well, for Pete's sake, you can leave the car on the mainland.

"I can?" Sam asked, as if the idea had never once occurred to him.

"Of course. Look, Sam—"

The door opened. Zach turned to face it. Lieutenant Whitson was standing in the doorway.

"Is that your lawyer?" he asked.

"Yes."

"Tell him to forget it. We're letting you go."

"What?"

"You heard me. Tell him."

Zach told him. Sam seemed puzzled but relieved. He advised Zach to get the hell back to New York as fast as he could, and then he hung up. Zach cradled the phone and turned to Whitson.

"This is a surprise. What happened?"

Whitson shrugged. "I sent some men down to your beach this morning at dawn. We found your tomahawk."

"And that's why you're letting me go?"

Whitson studied him for a moment. "I'll level with you, Mr. Blake," he said.

"Go ahead."

"I knew you didn't kill her. I knew it when we picked you up. You've got brown hair, and the dead woman was holding a fistful of blond hair. But you *did* go there to see her, and I wanted to know why. I still wish you'd tell me."

"I can't," Zach said honestly.

"Okay, have it your way. You could save us a lot of trouble."

"I'm sorry."

"Sure. You're still not entirely in the clear, Mr. Blake. You might remember that. A lot of things about this case stink to high heaven—and you're one of them."

"What are the others?"

"The woman's husband and son. They've both disappeared."

"Where to?"

"We don't know. His boat is still at the dock, so he didn't take to the water. There're a lot of woods on the island. He may be hiding out in the brush. We'll find him. Sooner or later, we'll find him."

"What makes you think he's hiding from *you*? He may be afraid of whoever killed his wife. Did that occur to you?"

"Mr. Blake, a lot of things occur to a man who deals

with crime and evil. A lot of things.'' Whitson was silent for a moment, staring at the floor. ''Do you know what I wish?''

''What?''

''Even though it would mean losing my job, I wish there were no such thing as evil.'' He smiled grimly. ''But even the wicked may come, the man said. I guess he was right.''

''What are you talking about?''

''I'm talking about the Vineyard. Do you know what really started it as a summer resort?''

''No. What?''

''The Methodist Camp Meeting in Oak Bluffs. An annual religious meeting, Mr. Blake, which became the largest in the world. They used to pitch tents, but after a while too many people were coming and they had to find lodging elsewhere, away from the Tabernacle. This is a good island, Mr. Blake. Warm days and cool nights, the sea, the smell of bayberry and blackberry, the mild air. People came for the camp meeting and stayed on after the Parting and the Sacrament. They told other people about it, and pretty soon folks were coming here to enjoy the island itself, with no religious ideas at all. That's when the man made his observation.''

''What observation?''

''His name was Hebron Vincent. He said, 'Even the wicked may come, as they are likely to appear anywhere, but the visit is bound to be good for them.' ''

''I see.''

''Even the wicked may come, Mr. Blake. That's why we get murder, maybe. That's why I've got a job.''

''I wish I could help you,'' Zach said.

''You can. Why'd you go to see Evelyn Cloud?''

Zach did not answer.

''What are you afraid of, Mr. Blake?''

''Nothing.''

''Then tell me.''

''I can't.''

Whitson sighed. "Okay. Get out of here. The door's open." He paused. "Where can I find you if I need to?"

"In New York. I'm catching the 1:45 ferry."

"Don't be ridiculous, Mr. Blake."

"What?"

"I told you you're still not out of this, and you're not."

"What do you—?"

"I'm telling you not to leave the island. Not at 1:45, and not until we wrap this up. Do you understand?"

"I've *got* to leave!"

"Why?" Whitson snapped. Zach didn't answer. "Okay. You'll be watched. Don't try to board that ferry. So long, Mr. Blake."

The troopers drove him to Menemsha. He thanked them and went into the house. Everything was as he'd left it. He looked at his watch. It was close to nine, still five hours before the 1:45 P.M. ferry. He had no intention of heeding Whitson's warning. He would board that ferry if he had to fight every cop on the island to do it. He wondered if he should begin packing. And then he wondered why John Cloud had taken to the woods, and he remembered the fright in the big Indian's eyes. He looked at his watch again. There was still time, a lot of time, before he had to board the ferry. He closed the door and went out to the car. A note was pinned to the steering wheel. It read:

Zach—

I tried to get you several times on the phone, and finally came over. Your car is here, but no sign of you. I can't imagine what's happened. I'm a normal worrier, but this time I'm frantic. After last night and Penny, I don't know what to think. Will you call me as soon as you return? Please!

Enid

He tore the note from the wheel and went into the house. In the pantry, the number he'd left for Thelo the night before was still resting alongside the telephone. He dialed it and listened while the phone rang on the other end.

"Hello?" The voice was clipped and precise, a voice speaking careful English, but nonetheless marked with a German accent.

"Hello, may I speak to Enid, please?"

"She is not here right now. Who is this, please?"

"Zachary Blake. Is that you, Dr. Reutermann?"

"Who?"

"Dr. Reutermann?"

"No."

"Oh, I thought—"

"This is the cleaning woman. Miss Murphy is not here right now."

"Do you know where she is?"

"She went to the newspaper office."

"Thank you. Tell her I called. And tell her I'm all right."

"Yes, I will."

"Thank you."

He hung up and went out to the car, puzzled. The woman had sounded exactly like Dr. Reutermann. He remembered her talk of the proposed Nike site, her intimations of a spy melodrama. I'm being ridiculous, he told himself, but for God's sake, isn't the Nike a secret weapon, and hasn't my daughter been kidnaped, and doesn't this whole goddamn thing stink of guys in beards carrying bombs?

Did Mary see something?

Did Mary hear something?

How did my wife Mary, who was on her high school swimming team, who helped bring that high school to a city championship in 1939, drown?

He had asked the question over and over again last year, and now he was asking it again, and there was still no answer.

And so he started the car and backed out of the drive,

and as he went to Gay Head, he kept thinking of the Nike site, and he kept thinking that the cleaning woman who had answered the phone had sounded remarkably like Dr. Inge Reutermann.

11

THE CLOUD HOUSE LOOKED DIFFERENT TODAY. IT LOOKED gayer, even though it had been visited by death. The sun was shining today, and it caught at the gray shingles of the house, caught at the scattered paint buckets on the front porch and the brilliantly decorated stone heads of the souvenir tomahawks.

There was no sign of life about the house. The police, the medical examiners, the laboratory technicians, the photographers—all had apparently come and gone.

Zach did not know what he was looking for. He had come here on impulse, and now that he was here he felt somewhat foolish. Had he hoped to find Cloud or the boy? He didn't know.

He sighed, got out of the car, and walked to the house. The front door was unlatched. He went inside. The house was very still, very empty. In the living room, the police had chalked an outline of Evelyn Cloud's body on the wood floor and a dark brown stain had saturated the wood near the chalked head. A blood stain and a chalk outline, he thought. That's all that's left of an Indian woman who tried to help me. And her husband has run away—and why?

Because he's scared.

Scared of what?

Scared of an international spy ring trying to steal the plans for the Nike.

It didn't sound plausible. How would an Indian swordfisherman get involved with spies? No, it sounded wrong. But what sounded right? He looked around the room, trying to visualize Evelyn Cloud fighting off her blond attacker, ripping the medallion from his neck, and then succumbing to the blows of the tomahawk.

Enid Murphy was a blonde.

So was Peter Rambley, the real estate salesman.

And so was Freddie Barton who was here for the express purpose of sailing his Raven in the regatta tomorrow.

How many blonds are there on Martha's Vineyard? Zach wondered. How many blonds are capable of committing murder? He shrugged, looked around the room again, and despondently went out to the kitchen.

The dish towel surprised him because he was certain the police would not have left it here. And yet it hung on the towel rack over the sink, the large smear of blood on it bright and red. He shook his head wonderingly, and then he stepped closer to the towel. There was a peculiar smell in the kitchen, the smell of . . .

Turpentine?

Of course. The painting Evelyn Cloud did, the souvenir tomahawks. He took the dish towel from the rack and smelled the stain. Paint. Not blood, but paint. He smiled. Things had come to a pretty pass when you automatically assumed paint was blood. But had the towel been here yesterday? He tried to reconstruct his entrance into the kitchen on the afternoon he'd found the body. Surely he'd have seen something with such a bright red stain. And if the towel had not been there then, had the paint been wiped onto it later? Last night? And by whom? John Cloud? Before he fled with the boy?

But why?

Red paint.

There were buckets of paint on the front porch. Zach dropped the towel and went out there. At least a dozen cans of paint rested among the painted tomahawk heads. There were four cans of red paint. But only one of them had a screwdriver lying alongside it. He picked up the screwdriver and pried the sticky lid from the can. It was full almost to the top with the same bright red paint that had been on the dish towel. Had John Cloud opened this same paint can last night or early this morning? The paint looked untouched. He looked at the brushes lying on a piece of canvas on the wooden floor of the porch. They had all been cleaned thoroughly. None of them were stained with red paint. Then if John Cloud had not done any painting, why *had* he opened this can? Or had he painted and then simply cleaned his brush?

On a dish towel?

Why not? He had wiped his hands clean on it, hadn't he? Again, Zach allowed his eyes to roam over the porch. Paint rags, soiled and multicolored, lay on a table at the far end of the porch. He went to them. None of them had been used recently, certainly not this morning. John Cloud had wiped off a smear of red paint, and he had wiped it onto a dish towel. Unless the man were an absolute slob, the act seemed to indicate a man in a hurry. But how had he got the paint on himself? The lid. Of course. It was impossible to touch it without smearing red paint onto the hand.

Zach went back to the can of red paint. On impulse, he thrust the blade of the screwdriver into the can. He felt it strike something. He prodded the depths of the paint again. There was something stiff and unyielding inside the can. He dropped the screwdriver, rolled up his sleeve, took off his watch, and reached into the can. His hand came out dripping with red paint, holding a rectangular-shaped package. Zach dropped the package to the canvas and tried to untie the heavy cord around it. The cord was wet, and difficult to manage. He went back into the kitchen, wiped his hand on the dish towel, and then found a knife in the kitchen-table drawer.

His fingers were trembling as he cut the cord. He unfolded the soggy brown wrapping paper carefully. The wrapping paper concealed an oil-skin pouch, and he wondered for a moment why a tobacco pouch was immersed in a can of paint, and then he unwound the pouch, reached into it, and found another packet of wrapping paper, this one untouched by the red paint. He cut the cord on it, and opened it. His eyes widened in surprise.

He was looking at forty-five-thousand dollars in one-thousand-dollar bills.

And at that instant, he heard the automobile coming up the dirt road.

12

He froze.

His first thought was that it might be the police coming back. He'd been lucky this morning, but perhaps his luck was running out. If they threw him into the pokey again, how could he get off the island? He had to get on that 1:45 ferry, had to be seen boarding it, had to be in Providence by 5:00. If this was the police . . .

Hastily, he thrust the tobacco pouch into his trousers pocket. The car was closer now. He walked quickly to the table with the paint rags, unscrewed the cap on a bottle of turpentine, and poured it liberally onto his hand. He was wiping off the remaining traces of the red paint when the car pulled up. It was not a police car. He rolled down his sleeve, strapped on his watch, and calmly stepped off the front porch.

The girl in the car was Anne Dubrow.

She got out of the car, her short black hair tight against her head, the sea-green eyes alert. She walked stiffly erect, the way her mother did, a woman of purpose.

"What are you doing here?" she said.

"I was about to ask you the same thing."

"We rent this house to the Clouds," Anne said. "After what happened . . ." She shrugged. "I imagine we'll be looking for new tenants. I came to inspect the place."

"Is that why you came?" Zach asked.

"Yes. You sound as if you don't believe me."

"What's there not to believe?" Zach said.

"You're a funny guy. And I don't mean funny haha."

"Am I?"

"Your wife drowned, okay. Stop acting as if everybody on the Vineyard held her head under water."

"Maybe somebody on the Vineyard did," Zach said.

"Sure. And maybe I'm a Martian who—"

"My wife was a high school swimming champ," Zach said. "She went down to the beach *three* hours after breakfast, and she'd never had a cramp in the water in all the time I'd known her."

"The currents in Menemsha Bight are tricky," Anne said.

"That's what they told me last year. But I'm beginning to think a lot more than the currents are tricky."

"Meaning?"

"Meaning somebody *may* have held her head under water."

"If you believe that, why don't you go to the police?"

"Thanks, but I'd rather not."

"What are you doing here?"

"I wanted to look around," Zach said.

"For what?"

"What would I be looking for?"

Anne's eyes did not leave his face. Shrewdly, they studied him. "I don't know," she said slowly. "I'm asking *you.*"

Zach shrugged.

"Where's your daughter?" Anne asked. Her eyes were still narrowed. Suspiciously, she watched him.

"On the mainland."

"Where?"

"Don't you know?"

If he had intended to trap her, he was sadly disappointed.

"How would I know?" she asked, her eyes wide now.

"I thought everybody knew everything about everybody on the Vineyard."

"If you dislike it so much," Anne said, "why the hell don't you go back where you came from?"

"You've been trying to get me to do that since the moment I arrived,'' he said. ''Relax. I'm leaving on the 1:45 boat. You can give the damn cottage to your Mr. Carpenter.''

''Are you kidding?'' Anne asked.

''I'm dead serious.''

''But you paid for the cottage,'' she said.

''Oh? You're sure about that now?''

''I called Mother in Boston last night. She said you'd wired her the money, and she said Pete Rambley was a fool.''

''That sounds like your mother,'' Zach said.

''Well, if Mr. Carpenter takes the house, I'll refund your $500,'' Anne said. ''That's the least I can do.''

''That's the nicest thing anyone has said to me since I got here,'' Zach said.

Anne's face softened. ''It's not a bad place,'' she told him. ''It gets very dreary in the winter, but it's not a bad place. I'm sorry you didn't enjoy yourself.''

''I suppose I prejudiced myself against it,'' he said, watching her face. ''I was in the Air Corps during the war, and I understand the Air Force is moving into the island.''

''Is it?''

''Yes. Don't you know about it?''

''About what?''

''They're installing a Nike-launching site. I thought everybody knew that.'' He watched her carefully.

Anne Dubrow stared at him blankly. ''A *what* launching site?''

''Nike,'' he said.

''A night-key-launching site? What's that?''

''Nike,'' he repeated. ''It's a guided missile with a warhead. Haven't you ever heard of the Nike rocket?''

''No.'' She thought about it for a moment. ''I don't see why it should have disturbed you, anyway. You're a funny guy. Nike.'' She shrugged. ''You must have really disliked the Air Corps.''

''I wouldn't go back into it for forty-five-thousand dollars,'' he said.

Anne laughed lightly. ''Maybe you *are* funny haha. Maybe we hicks don't appreciate your humor.''

''Maybe not,'' he said. ''Well, I'll be running along now. I hope you find what you're looking for.''

''All I'm looking for are damages we'll have to repair before we rent again. That's all.''

''How about the money?'' he said.

Anne blinked. ''What money?''

He hesitated before answering her. Her eyes looked completely guileless, but he could not be certain. ''My five hundred dollars,'' he said. ''Will you know where to send it?''

Again she laughed. ''I admire a cold-hearted businessman,'' she said. ''Where do you *want* me to send it?''

''Resignac Broadcasting in New York,'' he told her.

He went to the car and started it. Anne Dubrow walked onto the front porch, looked briefly at the paint cans, and then went into the house.

''Night key,'' he murmured, and drove off.

13

HE PACKED IN THE SILENCE OF THE MASTER BEDROOM. HE had packed in this same room, in a deeper silence, the year before. The year before, each piece of Mary's clothing in the dresser drawer had been a physical reminder of her. Torturously, he had packed the bags and then had driven to the ferry.

This year, he packed Penny's clothes, the sun suits and the dresses and the bathing suits and sneakers and dungarees. And with each garment, he thought of his daughter, and he longed for 1:45 P.M., willed it to come quickly, desperately wished the time would pass swiftly. He broke the time into segments so that, compartmentalized, it seemed shorter. It would take him a half-hour to drive to Edgartown. If Lieutenant Whitson was still there, he would give him the forty-five-thousand dollars he'd found at the Cloud house. If not, he would leave it with the Edgartown police. Or was it wise to go anywhere near the police? In any case, he would have to leave Menemsha at about a quarter to one if he wanted to catch that boat. What time was it now?

He glanced at his watch. 9:45. Three hours before it was time to start. Four hours before he boarded the boat. And then the long ride to Providence. Was Penny all right? Or had they already . . . ? Could they do something like that, could they ruthlessly . . . ?

He refused to think about it. Penny was all right. She would be waiting in Providence at a restaurant called . . .

For a moment, his mind went blank.

What was the name of the restaurant?

God, what . . . ?

The blue . . .

The Blue . . .

Think! his mind shrieked. For God's sake, think! What had he said? What was the name of . . .

The Blue Viking!

He sighed and sat on the edge of the bed. He lighted a cigarette, watching his trembling hands, telling himself he had to keep his grip until this was all over, until Penny was safe in his arms again. He smoked, relaxing as he did. Again he looked at his watch.

It was 9:50.

Had only five minutes passed?

How could he possibly live until five o'clock this afternoon, knowing that Penny was in the hands of strangers, knowing that her life depended . . .

Don't!

Don't even think it. Just relax. It'll be all right. She'll be there. She'll be waiting for you at the restaurant. She'll see you, and she'll come running to you, and she'll smile, and her smile will be the radiant smile of Mary, and you'll hold her close and comfort her, comfort her.

"The Blue Viking," he repeated aloud, afraid he would forget it again, wanting to commit it irrevocably to memory.

He took the remainder of her clothing from the drawer, and then closed the suitcase. The lock would not snap. He tried it again. The suitcase was packed full, and one clasp wold certainly not hold it shut. He left the bedroom and went into the corridor inside the front entrance, opening the closet door there, looking for a toolbox. All he needed was a screwdriver to force the spring back into place. There was no toolbox in the closet. He checked each closet in the house, and then tried to fix the spring with a kitchen knife. Cursing, he realized he needed not only a screwdriver but a pair of pliers. Didn't Mr. Fielding keep any tools whatever in his damned house? Where would he keep tools? In the basement, where else? Zach went out of the house and threw open the cellar doors, starting down the steps.

A huge spider web had been woven across one corner of the stone overhang that formed the cellar ceiling. He ducked beneath it, saw a hanging light just beyond the web, and turned it on. The right-hand side of the cellar was stacked from floor to ceiling with shakes and cut logs, fuel for the fireplace in the living room. The hotwater furnace was over on the left of the basement, and beyond that was a row of floor-to-ceiling shelves. Zach walked over to them.

Mrs. Fielding, whoever she was, was both an industrious and a farsighted woman. The shelves were covered with preserves she had undoubtedly made herself and put into Mason jars. In addition, there were rows and rows of canned goods, boxes of candles, tinned biscuits, and at least a dozen jars of what looked like floor or sugar. Curiously, Zach unscrewed the lid of one of the big jars, dipped his finger into it, and tasted it. It was sweet. Sugar then. Mrs. Fielding was apparently expecting a new war with its ensuing sugar rationing. A new war with its . . .

And again Zach thought of the Nike site.

He screwed the cup back onto the jar, placed it with the other big jars of sugar, and searched the remaining shelves for a toolbox. He did not find it on the shelves, but he did find it resting on a suitcase in one corner of the basement. He opened it, took out a screwdriver and a pair of pliers, turned out the light, avoided the spider web, and left the cellar of the sugar-hoarding Mrs. Fielding.

He was reclosing the cellar doors when the car pulled up in front of the house.

"Zach!"

He recognized Enid Murphy's voice at once. He let the second door slam shut and then turned to greet her, surprised to discover he was smiling. The smile dropped from his face when he saw she had company. The man walking from the car with her was Freddie Barton, the regatta champ.

"Putting up some preserves?" Freddie asked.

"Just a few to get me through the winter," Zach answered. Enid ran to him and took his hand.

"I was worried sick," she said. "Have you heard anything further?"

"No."

"What are you going to do?"

"Leave," he answered.

Freddie Barton walked over to where they were standing. "Nice house," he said. "Good view of the water."

"Yes," Zach said. "Why don't you go out on the porch? The view's better from there."

Freddie's eyebrows went up speculatively. "You two want to be alone?" he asked.

"Yes," Enid answered.

"Sure," Freddie said, apparently amused. "Just call me Cupid." He walked around the side of the house, and they could hear his shoes clattering on the steps as he climbed to the porch.

"Where were you?" Enid said. "I kept calling and calling—"

"I was in jail. Look, did you check on—"

"In jail?"

"Yes. Did you check on that regatta date?"

"This morning," Enid said. "It was held on July 13th last year."

Zach nodded.

"Is it important, Zach?"

"I guess not."

"What do you mean?"

"Mary drowned on the 25th."

"What possible connection could there be, anyway?"

"I don't know."

They stood silently looking at each other.

Enid broke the silence. "You said you're leaving. Without Penny?"

"I'm to pick her up in Providence."

"Will you come back?"

"Why?" he said.

She took his hand in her own. Very softly, very gently, she said, "Because I want you to, Zach."

"Why?"

"You'll think I'm silly."

"No, I—"

"You'll think I'm reckless and—"

"No—"

". . . shameless and . . . and . . . a Merry Widow."

"What, Enid?"

"It would mean a great deal to me, Zach. If you come back."

He looked at her and there was expectation on her face, and anticipation, and the anticipation was somehow pained, as if she expected to be injured.

"You . . . you hardly know me," he said.

"I know you, Zach Blake," she answered.

"I'm . . . I'm not a very nice guy. I go around long-faced, and I—"

"You're a nice guy," she said. "You're a very nice guy," and she kissed him. He clung to her this time. He clung to her because she was a woman, soft and sweet-smelling, and he clung to her because there was another need inside him, a need to love and be loved, a need to call something his own, perhaps to call this woman his own. She broke from him, but her fingers held to his arms.

"You'll come back," she said.

"I'll see."

"You'll come back," she repeated.

They heard Freddie's footsteps coming around the side of the house. She pulled back her hands, but her eyes lingered on his face.

"A view's a view," Freddie said. "How long can I keep looking at it?"

"When are you leaving, Zach?" Enid asked.

"I've got to catch the 1:45 ferry."

"You going to Vineyard Haven?" Freddie said.

"Yes."

"Mind if I go along with you?"

"I won't be leaving until later."

"That's all right. I'm in no hurry."

He studied Freddie. The voice on the telephone had said a man would be watching in Vineyard Haven, to make sure he boarded the ferry. Was Freddie Barton that man?

"I don't want to seem rude," Zach said, "but I'd rather go alone."

"Sure," Freddie said. He smiled indulgently. "I'll find my way there. Maybe I'll run into you."

"Maybe you will."

"Sure," Freddie said. "Maybe I will." He turned to Enid. "Want to drop me off at the tennis courts, sugar? I'm a half-hour late already."

"Will you call me from Providence, Zach?" Enid asked.

"All right."

She took his hand and squeezed it. "Be careful."

"I will," he promised.

At 10:30 he went down to the docks again.

Looking out over the waters, he wondered how it had been for Mary last year. How do you drown? How does an expert swimmer drown? Is it quick, is it painless? Or do you struggle against a strong pair of hands holding you under?

Your wife Mary did not drown accident.

"The currents are very tricky in the Bight, Mr. Blake. You wife shouldn't have gone out so far."

Mary dead, his mind echoed dully. *Mary dead.*

"Perhaps she suffered a cramp, Mr. Blake. Perhaps that's what happened."

And his mind had repeated, *Mary dead, Mary dead, Mary dead.*

Now, as he looked out over the waters, there was no feeling of menace. As still as a lake, the water reflected a flawless blue sky. A boat with red sails lay becalmed far out near the Elizabeth Islands. It was a beautiful day, and more beautiful down at the docks where the real life of an island throbs in muted regularity. He could understand why people came here—*even* the wicked. He could understand.

He would not have recognized Cloud's boat had he not seen the name *Evelyn* painted on the prow. It was a trim fishing craft, painted a light blue, with the dead woman's name lettered onto it in black paint. He walked to the boat. A muscular man wearing only a tee shirt was working on the engine. A cigar jutted from one corner of his mouth. The man chewed relentlessly on the cigar, oblivious to the fact that it was dead.

"Al right to come aboard?" Zach said.

The man looked up. There was a faint beard stubble on his face. A curious-looking scar curled on his right cheek. He took the cigar out of his mouth, studied Zach for a moment, and then said, "Who's asking?"

"Zach Blake."

"You own this boat?"

"No."

"What's your business on her?"

"I wanted to talk to you."

"What about?"

"I'd rather talk aboard."

"Come ahead then."

Zach leaped from the dock to the boat. He looked for a place to sit, pulled up a fender and straddled it while the man went back to the engine. The man's hands were powerful, but he poked at the engine with the delicacy of a surgeon.

"You're aboard," he said without looking up, "so start talking."

"Do you know John Cloud?"

"Nope."

"Then what are you doing on his boat?"

"I was hired."

"What for?"

"To take her out."

"For what?"

"Fish, I guess. Why else would you take out a fishing boat?"

"Who hired you?"

"Fellow in Oak Bluffs. I'm a fisherman. My boat was smashed in the last hurricane. A fisherman without a boat is dead. I hire myself out sometimes. I'm building a new boat now, but it takes time."

"What was the name of the man who hired you?"

"Why do you want to know?"

"I'm curious."

"You sound *too* curious. I got this scar being curious. Fellow on my boat once made a strike. I couldn't wait to see the damn fish. I leaned over the side while he was pulling her in. The fish got off the hook, and the hook snapped up and caught my cheek. It don't pay to be too curious, mister."

"Maybe not. Who hired you?"

"I don't suppose I'll tell you that until I know why you want to know," the man said.

"Do you want money? Is that it?"

"I make my money fishing." The man paused. "There's a name for people who sell information. I don't like the name."

"There's a name for people who withhold it, too," Zach said.

"Suppose you just tell me why you're interested."

The man looked up, chewing his cigar. Zach met his eyes.

"My wife drowned here last year," he said. "I don't believe it was an accident. Is that a good enough reason?"

"That's a pretty good reason," the man said. He extended his hand. "They call me Ahab because of the scar. My real name's Abraham."

Zach took his hand. "Which do you prefer?"

"Either one. I'll answer to either or both. I remember the drowning. Martha. Wasn't that her name?"

"Mary," Zach said.

"Mary, yep. You still want to know who hired me?"

"Yes."

"A fellow named Carpenter."

"In Oak Bluffs, you said?"

"Yes."

"Where'd he hire you? Does he have an office or something?"

"Nope. Said he had a boat and needed somebody to take him out in it tomorrow. Said he'd asked around and heard I was a good sailor." Ahab paused. "I am."

"Where was this?"

"A bar. Right opposite the carrousel. You familiar with Oak Bluffs?"

"No."

"Well, there's an Italian restaurant on the corner, just as you come into town. Sort of a circle there. The carrousel's across the street from that in this wooden building. And the bar's right alongside the restaurant. That's where he found me." Ahab paused again. "I drink a lot."

"What's the man's first name?" Zach asked.

"Carpenter. That's all I know."

"What time are you going out tomorrow morning?"

"Early."

"How far out?"

"He didn't say."

"Fishing?"

"I suppose so. Why else would you take out a fishing boat? This ain't exactly a pleasure cruiser."

"How much is he paying you?"

"That's personal, ain't it?" Ahab said.

"I suppose so. It's not important. Forget it. And thank you."

"My pleasure," Ahab said. He took Zach's hand again. "I've got a wife too, Mr. Blake. Good luck."

"Thanks," Zach said. He leaped to the dock, and as he began walking, Ahab called after him, "He's paying me thirty dollars a day."

14

IF EVERY COMMUNITY MUST HAVE A CONEY ISLAND, THEN Oak Bluffs was the Coney Island of Martha's Vineyard.

Zach entered the town at about 11:00 in the morning, passing the boats moored in the water on the left. The first sign that he was entering a carnival town was the multitude of paddle boats on the water. The boats were strictly for the amusement-park trade, and no respectable seaman would have come within ten feet of them.

As he proceeded into the town looking for a parking space, he was amazed by the number of bars on each street. He knew that Oak Bluffs and Edgartown were the only two "wet" communities on the island, but he felt nonetheless that Oak Bluffs was trying a little too desperately to outdo its dry neighbors.

He parked three blocks away from the carrousel and began walking back down the main street. The street was crowded, and he might have missed the boy behind him had he not been wearing a bright orange shirt. But the lurid shirt caught his eye, and as he walked past the hot-dog stands and the ice-cream stands and the cotton-candy stands, he became increasingly certain that the boy in the orange shirt was following him. In spite of what had happened since he'd come to the Vineyard, the idea of being followed in this gingerbread-house town was somehow ludicrous. He walked rapidly past the Indian restaurant on the corner, turned right, and found the bar in which a man named Carpenter had hired Ahab. He hesitated outside for just a moment, and then entered. The boy in the orange shirt came in a moment later.

A fishing net had been draped over the mirror behind the bar. The room was long and narrow. Two men, both wearing fishing boots, were playing shuffleboard. The bar top was chipped and scarred. Judging from the number of initials-in-hearts carved into the wood, Oak Bluffs was a very loving town. Zach pulled up a leatherette stool and sat. The boy in the orange shirt walked to the far end of the bar, sat, and ordered a beer. The bartender drew it, and then walked to Zach.

"Call it," he said.

"Rye neat," Zach answered. "And a man named Carpenter."

"I've got the rye," the bartender said. He hooked a shot glass with his forefinger, took a bottle from the shelf below the net, and poured. "Want a chaser?"

"Water. What about Carpenter?"

"Never heard of him. Are you a cop?"

"Do I look like one?"

"The bulls from Axel Center look like Harvard men." The bartender shrugged. "A guy comes in asking questions, he's either a bull or a hood. I don't cater to neither."

"I'm neither."

"Why do you want this Carpenter fellow?"

"I understand he's going out on a boat tomorrow. I wanted to do some fishing. Thought I'd go along with him."

"He's a big fisherman," the boy in the orange shirt said.

Zach turned to him. "You talking about Carpenter?"

"I don't know any Carpenter. I'm talking about you." The boy was smiling. He wore his hair in a high crown, with long black sideburns. His eyes were brown, cruel, with the incongruously long-lashed lids of a girl. His mouth was thin with the faint suggestion of a perpetual sneer hovering about the lips. He seemed no older than seventeen, but he was excellently built, the orange shirt stretched taut over bulging muscles which were undoubtedly the product of weight lifting.

"I'd advise you to mind your own business, sonny," Zach said.

"I don't take advice from strangers," the boy answered.

"Shut up and mind your own business, Roger," the bartender said.

"Did I pay for this beer?"

"That don't—"

"Don't go shoving at me, Bill. I don't like getting shoved."

"Big man," Bill said disgustedly, dismissing the boy. "If you're interested in hiring a boat, mister, there's plenty around. Does it have to be this Carpenter's?"

"No. But I thought you might know him."

"Strangers shouldn't go around asking questions," Roger said from the end of the bar.

"Why don't you take a walk?" Zach said.

Roger was silent for a moment. Then he nodded and said, "Maybe I will," and he rose from the stool quickly, paid for the beer, and walked out of the bar.

"He's trouble," Bill said. "A bad apple. Got a record."

"At his age?" Zach asked, surprised.

"He's nineteen. Don't get mixed up with him, or you'll have the cops down on your ears."

"That's the last thing I want right now."

"Then don't mess with Roger. Take my advice."

"Thanks, I will. You don't know Carpenter, huh?"

"Never heard of him, Sorry."

"That's all right. What do I owe you?"

He was paying the bartender when Roger came back into the bar. There were two other teenagers with him.

"Get your boat?" he asked Zach.

"No."

"Get your Carpenter?"

"No."

"That's a shame."

"Yeah."

Zach picked up his change and walked out of the bar. Glancing over his shoulder, he saw that Roger and his friends were following him. And, abruptly, he realized he was carrying forty-five-thousand dollars in his pocket.

He crossed the street, following the music of the calliope to a high wooden building. He walked into the building. The carrousel occupied half of the wooden structure, whirling monotonously. An extended wooden army reached toward the carrousel, bearing rings one of which was presumably gold. The riders were mostly teenage girls reaching for the gold ring each time they whipped past the extended arm. The girls were adept at the game. Each time a girl's turn at the arm came up, her hand would move in a rapid succession of winking snaps, yanking half a dozen rings from the mechanism before the carrousel whirled her past the arm. Monotonously, the carrousel rotated. Monotonously, the girls performed their sleight of hand with the rings. The calliope music filled the hollow shell of the building, creating a mock carnival spirit. Zach watched for a while and then walked over to the stands opposite the carrousel.

A man whipped cotton candy from the rapidly revolving metal bowl, spinning the pink fluff onto its white holders.

"I'm trying to locate a man named Carpenter," Zach said.

The man looked up. "I don't think I know him."

"He's a fisherman," Roger's voice said behind Zach. "This man is a fisherman, too. A big fisherman."

"I still don't know him," the cotton-candy man said. He turned his eyes away from Roger, as if recognizing him for what he was and not wanting to have anything to do with him.

"Thanks," Zach said. He turned. The three boys were blocking his path. "You're in my way," he said.

"Are we?" Roger answered.

"Come on," Zach said patiently.

"Where we going?"

"Get out of my way."

"Why, you can just walk around us," Roger said.

Zach felt his fists balling at his sides. He forced himself to relax, and then walked around the boys. Roger snickered behind him. He started for the door and heard the clatter of their boots on the wooden floor behind him.

He walked back toward the car, stopping in each bar he passed and asking for Carpenter. No one seemed to know the man. And each time he came into the street again, Roger and his friends were waiting.

He did not want trouble with teenage punks. It was almost 11:30. In a little more than two hours, he had to board the ferry. A street brawl with young hoodlums was not the thing to encourage—not with Penny waiting in Providence, not with her life depending on whether or not he boarded that ferry. Doggedly, he walked back to the car. He was turning the ignition key when Roger and his friends caught up with him.

Roger climbed onto the hood, straddling it. His two friends sat on the right fender. Zach rolled down his window.

"How about it, fellows?" he said.

"We want a ride," Roger answered.

"Get off the hood," Zach said.

"Take us for a ride, fisherman."

"I can't see with you on the hood."

"That's a real shame," Roger said.

Zach sighed, opened the door on his side, and started for Roger. He was no sooner out of the car than the boys on the right fender leaped off, opened the door opposite the driver's seat, and scrambled into the back of the car.

"Hey!" Zach said. "What the hell—?" He went back to the car. Leaning in past the wheel, he said, "Look, I don't feel like—"

He looked across the front seat. Roger was standing in the opposite doorway. A Smith and Wesson .38 caliber revolver was in his fist.

"Get in, fisherman," he said.

Zach stared at the gun.

"Get in, I said."

He got into the car.

"Close the door."

He closed it.

"Now give me the loot," Roger said.

"What are you talking about?"

"The forty-five grand."

"What forty-five grand?"

"You want us to *take* it from you, fisherman?"

"I haven't got it, so how can you take it?"

"Start the car," Roger said. "Drive straight through town, and then make a left. We'll find a place and then convince you."

Zach started the Plymouth, and then edged into the stream of traffic. On the sidewalks, the crowds bought souvenirs and hot dogs and cotton candy. Slowly, the car moved down the main street.

"There's a traffic cop at the intersection," Roger said. "No funny stuff. I know how to use this gun."

"Suppose I stop the car and yell?"

"I wouldn't try it."

"Why not? What have I got to lose?"

"Your life," Roger said.

"And yours, too," Zach said. "I'm gambling you're not that stupid."

"What do you—?"

Zach stopped the car and then pulled up the hand brake. The man behind him began tooting his horn almost instantly.

"Get moving!" Roger said. "Goddamnit, I'm warning you! Get this heap moving."

"Go ahead, shoot me," Zach said. "That cop'll be here in two seconds. Go ahead, dope. Shoot."

Roger hesitated. His face was covered with a fine film of sweat. From the back seat, one of the boys whispered, "Rog! The cop. He's coming over . . ."

"Get this car moving, you bastard!" Roger shouted.

The hand with the gun was beginning to tremble. The traffic cop was waving his hands as he approached the Plymouth. He was a big, red-faced man, sweat staining the blue shirt he wore. Containing his anger, his face getting redder as he came closer, he strode rapidly toward the car.

"You'd better—" Roger started.

"You'd better hide that gun," Zach said, and Roger instantly put the .38 in his pocket.

"All right, what the hell is this all about?" the cop said.

"I was just letting these boys out, officer," Zach answered politely.

"At the busiest corner in town? For God's sake, what the hell do you think—?"

"They were just getting out, officer," Zach said. "You'd better hurry, boys. We're holding up traffic."

"If you're getting out, get out!" the cop said. "Come on, hurry it up."

Roger threw a frustrated menacing look at Zach. Then he opened the door and left the car. The boys in the back seat hurried out after him.

"Okay, mister, move!" the cop said, and Zach put the car in motion instantly.

Over his shoulder, he called, "See you, Rog!" and then he made a left turn and gunned the car toward Edgartown.

15

ON THE DRIVE TO EDGARTOWN, HE TRIED TO PIECE THINGS together. The encounter with Roger seemed to indicate one thing clearly. He was no longer dealing with a simple thing. He was dealing with what seemed to be an organized group, a group which could afford to hire local talent to do its dirty work. And knowing this, he wondered how many of the local residents were involved in the death of Mary, the death of Evelyn Cloud, the kidnaping of Penny. Forty-five-thousand dollars was a lot of money, and murder had certainly been committed before for less. But what was a swordfisherman doing with forty-five-thousand dollars? And how had Roger learned about the money so quickly? Was Anne Dubrow involved in this? She had, after all, been the only person who'd seen him at the Cloud house that morning—and her reason for being there had seemed flimsy enough. But if she'd been there in search of money . . .

Wait a minute, he told himself. Start from the beginning. Do it logically. Do it simply. Add the facts.

Fact: My wife Mary drowned last year in Menemsha Bight.

Fact: A letter from Evelyn Cloud told me the drowning was not accidental.

Fact: Evelyn Cloud was killed by a blond wearing a regatta medal.

Fact: John Cloud fled with his son. But first he left forty-five-thousand dollars immersed in a can of paint.

Fact: Freddie Barton is a sailor.

Fact: Ahab has been hired to take out Cloud's boat tomorrow.

Fact: He was hired by a Mr. Carpenter, the same man who rented the Fielding house from Pete Rambley.

Fact: Roger knew I had the forty-five-thousand dollars, and tried to get it from me by force.

Fact: Whoever is behind all this wants me out of the Fielding house and off the island today.

Those are the facts. How do you add them? Why is the Fielding house important? Why does Carpenter, whoever he is, want the Cloud boat? What is that forty-five-thousand dollars going to buy?

The plans for the Nike site?

Is Dr. Reutermann involved in this? But damnit, just how secret *is* the Nike? Haven't they already shown films of it on television? And didn't I see . . . now hold it a minute . . . on the drive up, didn't I see a sign in one of the Massachusetts towns? Rhode Island? Somewhere along the way, didn't the sign read NIKE SITE, OPEN FOR INSPECTION? Didn't it read something like that? And if the site is open to the public, isn't it a little farfetched to assume that any of this is connected with the guided missile?

The Fielding house.

The Fielding house and water. Mary was killed by water, and Freddie Barton is a sailor, and Carpenter hired a sailor to man the Cloud boat. Why? Because Cloud has run off, obviously, and because it's important to get that boat out on the water tomorrow. What's out there? What the hell is out there on the water? What did Mary see or hear last year?

I'm on a carrousel, he thought. I'm reaching for the gold ring the way those teenage girls were a little while ago. I'm grabbing half a dozen rings each time I pass that wooden arm—but I can't catch the gold one.

He drove directly to the Edgartown Yacht Club.

The town was bustling with pre-regatta activity. The people in the streets were dressed in casual sailing clothes, carrying canvas bags under their arms or dangling on white lines. The race was in the air, the excitement of a keen competition, the excitement of skilled sailors pitting small craft against the ocean. The town was thronged with strangers, each hoping to share vicariously in the thrill of the race. He wondered what it was like to be a man like Freddie Barton, a man who roamed from regatta to regatta, a man who made the sea his life, a man who flitted from oceanside to oceanside searching out races.

The yacht club was the hub of the activity. If the town seemed frenzied, the club seemed on the verge of excited hysteria. Zach sought out the man in charge of the regatta committee, and then asked to see a list of the entrants in tomorrow's race. The man was hurried, but very obliging. He produced the formal entry list, and Zach searched the pages until he found a listing for BARTON, FREDERICK. The name of Barton's boat was *Inheritance*.

"Do you know this fellow?" he asked.

The committee chairman looked at the list. "Freddie Barton? Sure. Races here every year. Races everywhere, for that matter."

"Ever win?"

"Not last year," he said. "Year before that, he did. He's a good sailor. In the winter, he hits the Florida regattas. Sails everywhere. The Coast, Lake George, everywhere. He's a real sailor. It's in his blood. Where there's water, you'll find Freddie Barton."

"Must be pretty rich. To be able to do that, I mean."

"Not so rich," the man said. "In fact, Freddie's broke. His father's loaded, but Freddie's a black sheep. The old man won't give him a dime."

"Then how can he afford—"

"The Raven? He inherited it. One of his uncles left it to him. That's why it's called *Inheritance*. I think that's pretty clever, don't you?"

"Yeah. How does he make a living?"

"Search me."

"Does he spend a lot when he's in here?"

"Same as any other club member."

"I thought you said he was broke."

"Well . . . well, that's what he always says."

"But he buys drinks and dinners and pays his bills, huh?"

"Yes. Yes, he does." The man shrugged. "Maybe he's got stock or something."

"Maybe so," Zach said. "Thanks a lot."

"You down for the regatta?" the man asked.

"You might say that," Zach answered, and he left the club."

It was a little after noon. In an hour and forty-five minutes, he would have to board the ferry. He debated whether or not he should turn over the forty-five-thousand dollars to the police. He decided against it. The money had so far succeeded in smoking out Roger and his playmates. The money was important, and you couldn't spring a trap without bait. Besides, he was fairly certain the police were not following him, and he did not want to remind them that he existed. Satisfied with his decision, he started the car and began driving back toward the house to pick up his luggage.

A red-and-black car was parked in front of the house. He recognized it at once as Pete Rambley's.

The real estate salesman was sitting at the kitchen table. His hand was on the table, and there was a .45 automatic in it.

"Come in, Blake," he said.

Zach entered the kitchen. The screen door slammed shut behing him.

"What do you want, Rambley?"

"The money," Rambley said.

"What money?"

"The money John Cloud left in a can of red paint at his house."

"I don't know what you're talking about."

"I'll explain as quickly as I know how, Blake. I'm in no particular hurry, but this gun is. Cloud has taken off.

After what happened to his wife. I guess he's scared for his kid's safety. He wants out. So he's hiding somewhere."

"Wants out of what?"

"That's none of your business. All you have to know is that he sent a note before he took off. The note said he had hidden something that belonged to us in a can of red paint on his front porch. That something is forty-five-thousand dollars, Blake, and I want it."

"What makes you think I've got it?"

"Anne Dubrow saw you at Cloud's house this morning. It's our assumption you stumbled across the money. Now hand it over."

"Is Anne in this, too?"

"Anne is nowhere near it. She simply mentioned to me that she'd seen you there. Give me the money, Blake."

"How do you know I've got it on me?"

"I don't. I'd just as soon go through your pockets *after* you're dead."

"And if I'm not carrying it, you'd never find it then."

"Perhaps not. But I hate to think of what would happen to your darling daughter without Dad around to look after her."

Zach reached into his pocket and threw the tobacco pouch onto the table. Slowly, with the gun trained at Zach's middle, Rambley thumbed through the stack of bills, counting.

"All there," he said. "You're an honest man."

"What have you done with my daughter?" Zach said.

"That's right, you have a ferry to catch, don't you?" He rose. "You'd better catch it. Time and tide . . ."

"I want to get my bags."

"Get them. And then get out. And forget all about Martha's Vineyard, Blake. When you get back to New York, don't mention a word of this to anyone. If you do, we'll find your daughter again. And next time, we won't be so gentle."

"You're a—"

"Get your bags. I'll wait until you're gone."

Zach put the luggage into his trunk and drove off. At 1:30 P.M., he boarded the ferry to Woods Hole. He did not see any police cars, but an unmarked sedan followed him onto the boat. There were two men in the sedan. Both looked like Harvard men. He put them out of his mind. If they were cops, they were cops, and he didn't give a damn.

He drove as fast as he knew how from Woods Hole, but he didn't get to Providence until six o'clock that evening.

16

SHE WAS SITTING IN A BOOTH ALONE.

The seat was covered with blue leather, and her blond hair was very bright against the blue. She sat with her hands folded in her lap, patiently erect. She did not see him when he entered the restaurant, so that he had a moment to observe her unawares.

He looked at her, and for the first time in a year, he did not think she resembled Mary; he found joy in thinking only, *She is my daughter, she is Penny.* She saw him then, and the smile appeared on her mouth, and again it was not Mary's smile; it was Penny's, it was his daughter's. He rushed to her and clasped her into his arms, and she said, "Oh, Daddy, Daddy, I thought you weren't coming."

"Are you all right. Honey, did they hurt—?"

"I'm fine. Daddy, you're shaking. I'm all right."

He held her close, feeling weak all at once, unable to speak. He sat abruptly, still holding her, and when he spoke, all he could say again was, "Are you all right?"

"Yes. They were nice to me."

"Who, honey?"

"The men."

"Which men?"

"All three of them. The two who took me from the house, and the one who brought me here today."

"Start from the beginning, honey."

"Two men came to the house. Last night, while you were at the party."

"What were their names?"

"I don't know."

"What did they look like?"

"One was young with black hair and sideburns. The other one was blond."

Roger. The black-haired one was Roger. But the blond? Rambley, of course. Freddie Barton had been at Enid's party last night. Then who had made the phone calls? One of Roger's cronies? It was possible.

"Where'd they take you, honey?"

"Down to the beach. They had a boat there, Dad."

"Was it John Cloud's boat? Was the name on it 'Evelyn'?"

"I don't know. It was dark. We didn't go far, just down the beach a ways. They were having a lot of trouble. Neither of them seemed to know very much about boats. The dark one said they needed the Indian, and the blond one said he bet the Indian was gone for good. Anyway, they docked the boat, and then we got into a car and drove to the ferry." She paused. "Is this Providence? They said we were going to Providence."

"Yes, this is Providence."

"They were talking about the Indian all the way here."

"What did they say?"

"The dark one said they should never have trusted him with all that money. Suppose the Indian *was* gone for good? What about the money? They were very disturbed about the money."

"What else?"

"They were also disturbed about who would take the boat out. The blond one said that would be taken care of."

"You said there was a third man, honey. You said he brought you to the restaurant."

"Yes. They took me to a house last night, gave me something to eat, and then locked me in. This afternoon, the third man came to get me. He drove me here and said I should wait for you, that you'd come to pick me up. He was blond, too."

Barton? How was Barton involved in this? Or was the

third man the Mr. Carpenter whom no one seemed to know?

"What else did they say, honey? On the way to Providence?"

"Something about a ship, Daddy, and about the stuff being aboard."

"What stuff?"

"I don't know. They just said 'stuff.' Whatever it was, there was twenty pounds of it."

"Twenty pounds of what?"

"The stuff."

A ship, Zach thought. A ship with twenty pounds of "stuff" on it. Was the forty-five-thousand dollars going to buy that "stuff"? What kind of "stuff" brought forty-five-thousand dollars for twenty pounds? Gold dust? Diamonds?

A ship.

And Mary had drowned in Menemsha Bight.

Water.

And the Fielding house.

A ship. And a fishing boat.

Whatever Mary had seen last year, it was going to happen again this year.

And this year, *Zach* wanted to see it.

"Come on, baby," he said. "We're going to find an airport."

The chartered plane put down at the Edgartown Airport at 10:27. Zach paid the pilot and then found a phone booth. He took Penny into the booth with him, and rapidly dialed Enid Murphy's number.

"Hello?" the voice said. It was the same voice he had heard earlier, the voice with the German accent.

"Let me speak to Miss Murphy," he said.

"Just a minute."

He waited. When she came onto the phone, he said. "Who was that?"

"My cleaning woman. Why?"

"Never mind. Did you get it?"

"Yes. Where are you?"

"At the Edgartown Airport."

"Have you got a car?"

"I'm renting a Jeep as soon as I hang up," Zach said.

"All right. Can you meet me at the basin on Menemsha Pond?"

"Yes."

"I'll be waiting," Enid said. "Zach?"

"Mmm?"

"Please hurry."

"I will."

"Nothing else?"

"What do you want me to say?"

"You could say . . . you could say a lot of things."

"I'm working on them," Zach said. "I'll see you soon. You haven't discussed this with anyone, have you?"

"No."

"Good. I'll be there. Take care of yourself."

He hung up and then inquired about the rental of a Jeep. When he got the car, he and Penny hopped in, and they began the drive to Menemsha Pond. The sky overhead was studded with stars. It would be a good day for the regatta tomorrow.

Enid was waiting on a Chris-Craft cruiser. She wore a white raincoat buttoned to the throat, and a green kerchief held her blond hair. Zach doused the Jeep lights as soon as he saw her. He took Penny's hand and walked to the boat. Enid rushed into his arms, and he held her close, surprised that he did not feel guilty or embarrassed holding a woman in his daughter's presence.

"Tell me what's going on," Enid said. "Please, Zach."

"Let's get Penny to bed first," he said. "She's had a busy day." He picked up his daughter and carried her into the cabin, and when they had tucked her in, she asked to kiss Enid good night, too.

They sat on the deck, their backs to the cabin. The pond was still and black. The occasional fish broke the silence of the surface. On shore the crickets chirped incessantly.

There was a three-quarter moon hanging in the sky among the sparks of stars. They sat, and the water lapped gently against the sides of the boat, and they spoke in whispers because Penny was asleep.

"Did my call from Providence surprise you?" he asked.

"No. You promised you'd call. But if frightened me."

Zach was silent for a moment, thinking. "Did you get the binoculars?" he asked.

"Yes. A very good pair. The man I bought them from said they're old Army glasses. The lenses are coated so that they won't reflect sunlight."

"Good. Did anyone question you about renting the boat?"

"No. I told them I wanted to go fishing in the morning." She paused. "Zach?"

"Mmm?"

"Where *are* you going in the morning?"

"I don't know. I figure I'll lay offshore until Cloud's boat goes out. Then I'm going to follow it."

"To where?"

"To wherever a ship might pass."

"The Gay Head light?"

"Why do you say that?"

"Well, ocean ships use it as a landfall. On the way to the Cape Cod Canal to Boston."

"That's pretty far out. Mary wouldn't have been that far out. Unless—"

"What?"

"Unless something happened in the Bight. Maybe she saw the boat . . ." He shrugged, puzzled.

"What do you think is going to happen tomorrow?"

"I think Cloud's boat is going to transact some business with an incoming ship. I think forty-five-thousand dollars is going to change hands."

Enid whistled softly.

"I think a similar transaction took place last year, and I think Mary stumbled onto it and was drowned because of it. Freddie Barton may be a part of this, though I can't figure out how."

"Freddie?"

"Yes. Is the regatta course marked by buoys?"

"Yes."

"How does it work?"

"You know."

"No, I don't."

"The boats all jockey for position near the starting line. The racers are carrying stop watches. Fifteen minutes before the start, the committee boat raises a white cone, and the racers set their stop watches. Ten minutes before the start, a red cone goes up. Then, five minutes before the gun, they raise a blue cone. The boats begin maneuvering toward the starting line. A good sailor will cross the line right when that gun goes off. If he crosses it before the gun, he has to turn back and make another run."

"But the course *is* marked with buoys?"

"Yes."

"What happens if a boat goes outside the buoys?"

"What do you mean?"

"Well . . . what happens?"

"If she's in trouble, do you mean?"

"Possibly."

"The committee boat will probably go after her."

"Did you watch the regatta last year?"

"Yes."

"Freddie Barton was in it, wasn't he?"

"Yes."

"Did he go outside the buoys?"

"No. Not that I can recall. I think he finished fourth. He misjudged the start and had to go back. He lost a lot of time that way."

"Then the regatta *isn't* a part of it," Zach said.

"What do you mean?"

"Or is it?" Zach said. "Maybe it's just Barton's legitimate excuse for being where he's *supposed* to be. For being wherever that damn shipment is coming in."

"I don't know what you're talking about, Zach."

Zach smiled. "I'm not sure I know, either. Come on, you'd better get home."

"What time are you going out tomorrow?" Enid asked.

"Before sunup."

"I'm going with you. You know that, don't you?"

"There may be trouble."

"I don't care."

"All right."

"So . . . so I'd like to stay aboard tonight."

"Enid—"

"Zach, I don't want to leave you. I want to be with you. I . . . I want to be very close to you."

He did not answer for a moment. And then he put his arm around her and drew her to him. He kissed her throat and her ear and her jaw, and then he found her mouth, lost himself in the sweetness of her mouth, and then murmured against her lips, "Darling, darling," and the word sounded curious to him but he felt strangely alive again, alive for the first time in a very long while.

17

HE COULD SEE THE CLOUD BOAT THROUGH THE BINOCULARS from where he stood in the pilot house of the cruiser. He could see Ahab and another man, a blond man. He assumed the second man was Rambley.

"Are they coming out?" Enid asked.

"Yes. They're just getting under way."

They lay far offshore, the boat bobbing on a white-capped sea. The sun had been up for an hour, but there was still a cold nip on the air. Enid had taken off the white raincoat. She wore a green turtle-neck sweater and black slacks, and the wind tore at her blond hair, whipping it back over her shoulders. Penny sat cross-legged on the bow, looking out over the water.

"Zach, I'm . . . I'm frightened," Enid said.

"Don't be."

"I've got you now and . . . and I don't want to lose you. I couldn't take losing another . . . another . . ." She shook her head. "I'm sorry. I'm sorry. Forgive me, please."

"There's nothing to worry about."

"Isn't there?"

He did not answer. The Cloud boat was in the harbor now, heading on a direct course for the Gay Head light. Zach turned his binoculars seaward. On the horizon, clearly visible against the blue of the sky, was a freighter.

"So far, so good," he said. "Everything on schedule."

They waited. There was nothing to do but wait. As the Cloud boat approached, they went into the cabin. They did not emerge again until the Cloud boat was well past them. Zach raised the binoculars again. The Cloud boat and the freighter were on an apparent collision course.

"She's a French ship," he said. He lowered the binoculars. "Probably bound for Boston. She'll go through customs there, but by that time it'll be too late." He raised the glasses again. "Look! She's lowering a boat!"

Enid squinted at the horizon. The Cloud boat was maneuvering in a wide circle. The rowboat from the freighter edged closer, fighting the high whitecaps. Zach watched through the glasses. The exchange could not have taken more than five minutes. The Cloud boat swung around and headed back toward Menemsha. The rowboat turned toward the freighter.

"All over but the shooting," Zach said. "Has the regatta started yet?"

Enid looked at her watch.

"Yes."

"So Freddie Barton's clear and safe. Whatever they're smuggling in, Barton's regatta is the best alibi in the world. We're going to intercept that boat, Enid. You'd better get below."

"I'll stay here with you," she said. "Penny!"

Penny looked up. "Yes?"

"Come below, Penny," said Enid.

He watched his daughter. She obeyed Enid's command instantly. Enid took her hand and led her to the cabin. "Stay down there," she said, "no matter what happens. Do you understand?"

"Yes," Penny said solemnly.

"If anyone comes aboard, stay down there. Don't show yourself."

"All right," Penny said.

Enid smiled. "Now give me a kiss."

She hugged the child to her, and Penny returned her kiss. As she went below, she whispered, "Be careful."

"We will," Enid said. "Now not a sound."

The Cloud boat was approaching. Lowering the binoculars, Zach said, "It's Rambley, all right. Here we go, Enid. Hold tight."

He gunned the engine and then swung the boat sharply to port. Ahab, at the wheel of the Cloud boat, saw the sudden maneuver of the cruiser and instantly changed course. Zach swerved his boat again, heading directly for the fishing boat.

"Hey!" Ahab yelled across the water. "You damn idiot! What the hell are you . . ." and he swung the wheel again, trying to avoid the cruiser.

Like a wrestler circling for a hold Zach closed in on the other boat. "Get ready to take the wheel," he said to Enid. He circled aft of the fishing boat, crossing its wake, and then swinging in alongside the slower boat, matching its speed. "Now!" he shouted.

He gave the wheel to Enid, ran aft and then leaped across the narrow wedge of water to the deck of the smaller boat, coming to his feet instantly.

Rambley was waiting for him. The .45 was pointed at Zach's stomach.

"All right, Blake," he said. "You're asking for it."

"What'd you pick up out there?" Zach said.

"None of your damn business!"

"You're holding the gun," Zach said. "Are you afraid to talk even with a .45 in your hand?"

"I don't owe you a goddamn thing, Blake. You're going to—"

"What'd you get out there?"

"Heroin!" Rambley shouted. "Twenty pounds of heroin! You happy now? You can think about it while I pull this trigger."

At the wheel of the boat, Ahab's jaw went suddenly slack. He looked at Rambley and then at Zach, and his eyes opened wide in shocked recognition.

"Get over there with the sailor," Rambley said. "Hurry up. Against the wheel."

Zach moved to where Ahab stood. Alongside the fishing

boat, Enid maneuvered the cruiser, matching the speed of the smaller craft.

"What did you think this was, Blake?" Rambley asked. "A penny-ante game? Do you know what that twenty pounds'll bring us when we've cut it with sugar? A million and a half bucks. Even if this was a one-shot deal, it'd be worth it. You're messing with big money."

"What happened to my wife?"

"She drowned."

"Who drowned her?"

"She'd have drowned anyway," Rambley said. "She was in trouble, caught in the current. Cloud picked her up. I didn't even know she was aboard at first. I was down below, putting away the stuff, when he fished her out of the water. He put her on the deck and covered her with a blanket. I came topside and began talking about the heroin. He tried to shut me up, but I'd already said enough, and your damn wife heard every word."

"So you—"

"So I hit her and threw her over the side, yes! Did you think I was going to jeopar—"

Zach lunged forward. "You murdering son of a—"

"Hold it!" Rambley shouted. "Stay right where you are!"

Zach froze.

"Don't force it, Blake. You'll get it soon enough. The Indian woman forced it. Cloud never should have told her about it, never. But he did, and she forced it, and now she's dead. You should have stayed out of this. We gave you every chance to stay out of it, didn't we? You're a damn fool, Blake. And in three seconds you're going to be a dead fool. You and the sailor both!"

"Who's Carpenter?" Zach asked.

Rambley laughed, but did not answer.

"The Fielding house," Zach said suddenly. "The sugar in the basement, jars of it. Is that why you wanted me out?"

''That's where we're cutting and packaging the stuff, Blake. And once we've—''

''Enid!'' Zach shouted. ''Pull away! Get to shore!''

He saw the gun swing towards him, and he leaped forward. The explosion echoed on the water. He felt searing pain in his left shoulder, and then he slammed back against the side of the boat. He felt himself slipping to the deck, powerless to stop himself, saw the boards coming up, and then saw Rambley's sneakered feet as they turned from the wheel and closed in on him. He looked up into the open end of the .45. He sucked in a deep breath and waited. It was over now, it was all over.

And then Ahab left the wheel and hit Rambley from behind, and Zach saw Rambley collapse to the deck a moment before the pain in his shoulder claimed his consciousness.

18

THE HOSPITAL ROOM WAS VERY WHITE, AND IT SMELLED clean and antiseptic. Zach sat up in bed with his bandaged shoulder, and Lieutenant Whitson of Axel Center stood beside him and said, "You're a hero, Blake, and I hate to tell a hero it was all for nothing. But you could have saved yourself a bullet wound. We'd have cracked this without you."

"How?"

"We picked up the Indian this morning. In the woods off one of the pounds. He gave us all we needed."

"What'd he tell you?"

"He was their sailor, the only one other than Barton who could handle a boat. He's a swordfisherman and who suspects the comings and goings of a swordfisherman? What swordfisherman ever had to pass customs inspection? He was an ideal man for them. A good sailor who never roused any suspicion. They were going to send him out alone this year. That's why he was in possession of the forty-five grand."

"What happened?"

"They killed his wife. As simple as that. They killed the person he loved. He'd already been a witness to one murder last year, but this was something different."

"Yes."

"He didn't want any part of their operation any more. So he ran. But he knew he wouldn't be safe if he took their money with him. He left it for them, and sent them a note telling them where to find it. Apparently, you intercepted it. Why didn't you turn it over to me, Blake?"

"I was pretty much involved. I . . . I was afraid for my daughter."

Whitson nodded. "We'd have learned that, too, if you hadn't shaken my men in Providence."

"I wasn't trying to."

"You didn't have to. The damn Providence traffic took care of that."

"What about Carpenter? Did the Indian tell you about him?"

Whitson smiled. "There *is* no Carpenter. Carpenter is Barton and Barton is Carpenter. We picked him up right after the regatta. He came in second, he thinks."

"What do you mean?"

"He *really* came in last. He's the brains behind this whole thing, you know. Had this operation going on the Vineyard and similar ones wherever the hell there was a regatta. The regattas gave him a legitimate reason for being wherever his shipment was coming in. There's always a boat race somewhere, and there's always a ship coming in from someplace. He didn't even need exact timing. His damn races could be as much as a month before or after the shipment. It didn't matter. They provided the excuse for him to be near water, near the white gold that was coming in from all over the world."

"A shrewd cookie," Zach said.

"But not shrewd enough. He claims he's not involved in this at all. Wait until he sees the comparison tests we ran on his hair and the hair we found in Evelyn Cloud's fist."

"If you can get my clothes from the nurse," Zach said. "You'll find a regatta medallion in one of the pockets. I found it at the Cloud house. I imagine it's Barton's."

"Withholding evidence, huh, Blake?"

"There's also a kid named Roger who—"

"Roger's an old friend of ours. We've already got him behind bars."

Zach shrugged. His shoulder ached when he moved. "Then it's finished," he said. "It's all over."

"Except a thank-you to an honest sailor named Ahab who sure as hell knows how to swing a belaying pin. You might look him up when you get out of here."

"I will."

"Also, there are two young ladies waiting outside to see you. They're both blond, and they look sort of alike."

"One is my daughter," Zach said.

"And the other?"

"I hope she'll be my wife."

Whitson grinned. "In that case, I'll get the hell out of here." He stopped at the door. "Come back again, Blake. Maybe for your honeymoon, huh?"

He went out, and Zach leaned back against the pillows, grinning. Once upon a time, he thought, in the family called Blake, there was Penny and Enid and Zach. . . .

The door opened. Penny and Enid came into the room. And for the life of him, he didn't know which one to kiss first.